A WISH FOR FORGIVENESS

THE WISHING TREE SERIES, BOOK 14

AMANDA PROWSE

The Wishing Tree SERIES

PRAISE FOR AMANDA PROWSE

'Amanda Prowse is the queen of family drama' – Daily Mail
'A deeply emotional, unputdownable read' – Red
'Heartbreaking and heartwarming in equal measure' – The Lady
'Amanda Prowse is the queen of heartbreak fiction' – The Mail Online
'Captivating, heartbreaking and superbly written' – Closer
'Uplifting and positive but you may still need a box of tissues' – Cosmopolitan
'Powerful and emotional drama that packs a real punch' – Heat
'Warmly accessible but subtle . . . moving and inspiring' – Daily Mail
'Magical' – Now
A Wish for Forgiveness
The Wishing Tree Series, Book 14

The Wishing Tree SERIES

Amanda Prowse

Website: www.amandaprowse.com
Facebook: https://www.facebook.com/amandaprowsepage
X (formerly Twitter): @MrsAmandaProwse
Instagram: @mrsamandaprowse and @thechitchatters https://www.instagram.com/thechitchatters/
TikTok: https://www.tiktok.com/@amandaprowsewrites
Podcast Links: Chit Chat and All That

Published in the United Kingdom by Lionhead Media
ISBN 978-1-915400-07-9 (paperback)
ASIN B0CYHN4JLF (eBook)
FIRST EDITION
Cover by Elizabeth Mackey Graphic Design
Printed in the European Union

For our wonderful readers in My Book Friends

ALSO BY AMANDA PROWSE

NOVELS

Poppy Day

What Have I Done?

Clover's Child

A Little Love

Will You Remember Me?

Christmas for One

A Mother's Story

Perfect Daughter

The Second Chance Café

Three and a Half Heartbeats

Another Love

My Husband's Wife

I Won't Be Home for Christmas

The Food of Love

The Idea of You

The Art of Hiding

Anna

Theo

How to Fall in Love Again; Kitty's Story

The Coordinates of Loss

The Girl in the Corner

The Things I Know

The Light in the Hallway

The Day She Came Back

An Ordinary Life

Waiting To Begin

To Love and Be Loved

Picking Up the Pieces

All Good Things

Very Very Lucky

Swimming to Lundy

NOVELLAS

The Game

Something Quite Beautiful

A Christmas Wish

Ten Pound Ticket

Imogen's Baby

Miss Potterton's Birthday Tea

Mr Portobello's Morning Paper

I Wish...

A Whole Heap of Wishes

A Wish for Forgiveness

COMPILATION OF ALL SEVEN NOVELLAS

Something Quite Beautiful

MEMOIRS

The Boy Between: A Mother and Son's Journey From a World Gone Grey (with Josiah Hartley)

Women Like Us (Autobiography)

CHILDREN'S STORYBOOKS

The Smile that went a Mile

Today I'm in Charge!

Child

A Little Love

Will You Remember Me?

Christmas for One

A Mother's Story

Perfect Daughter

The Second Chance Café

Three and a Half Heartbeats

Another Love

My Husband's Wife

I Won't Be Home for Christmas

The Food of Love

The Idea of You

The Art of Hiding

Anna

Theo

How to Fall in Love Again; Kitty's Story

The Coordinates of Loss

The Girl in the Corner

The Things I Know

The Light in the Hallway

The Day She Came Back

An Ordinary Life

CHAPTER 1

Verity Darby hummed a song she had just heard on the radio; in fact, mis-hummed would be more accurate, not that she gave a fig! Jack always teased her about her lack of musical skill, noting how she rewrote lyrics at will, sang gibberish to fill a gap, and added random notes into a perfectly decent tune. This was no surprise and put her in mind of her early school days back in London when the very sweet and obliging choir mistress, Miss Melathorpe, had given her permission to join the choir. Verity had been delighted, running home to tell her mum, who had been equally thrilled! Enjoying the coach trips, the rather rowdy rehearsal sessions and even the choir Christmas supper, Verity had loved every minute of it.

Her entry into the esteemed choral society, however, had been on one condition: that she never, ever actually sang, a request Miss Melathorpe had made while wincing, as if imagining the caterwauling disaster that might ensue if Verity failed to adhere to this one abiding stipulation. This she had observed diligently and, whilst the billboard charts might not be calling any time soon, her miming skills were second to none. She liked to remind her husband that she couldn't be good at everything and that he should be thankful that she was a fabulous chef, a loving wife and was willing to overlook his obsession with fishing … He usually went quiet after that.

How she loved him!

It was still one of life's blessings that, as she hurtled towards her mid-fifties, she could live this way. Peace, she decided, was the closest thing to heaven and that was certainly how she saw her life here in Linden Falls, peaceful and quiet. To wake each day and know such joy filled her with a contentment she had never known existed. She and Jack would laugh at how boring they were! They worked hard, ate meals grabbed together around the kitchen table, and, on the evenings she wasn't working, they shared a blanket on the sofa while watching a movie and snaffling popcorn, both clamped under the weight of Truffle, their golden retriever, who only seemed truly happy when she was in direct contact with them both.

The sun shone on this beautiful day, and she felt nothing but excited for whatever lay ahead. She and Jack had enjoyed breakfast together that very morning and even Truffle was in a tail-wagging kind of mood. With the keys in her hand and life pottering on around her, the gentle hum of slow traffic, birdsong, and the burble of happy conversation, she stopped and took a second to look at the imposing frontage of Claudine's Bistro, and her face broke into a smile.

It had felt like an easy decision to take over the business when Claudine announced she was moving away. Although why anyone would move away from Linden Falls was quite beyond her! The two women had become great friends, working side by side for their monthly supper club and laughing hard and often at nothing much - in the way that great mates did. When the surprise at her friend's decision to quit had settled, and after no more than a cursory chat, an evening thrashing out the financials with Jack, and an in-depth conversation with the bank, Verity had taken out a loan to make her dream come true. All these years later, ownership of the place had not lost any of its sparkle. She was as excited by it now as she had always been.

It was hard to believe that it was nearly seven years since she had first wandered the town square of this beautiful small town, cloaked in self-consciousness and feeling like a Brit abroad. Instantly, she had been enamoured with the quaintness of the architecture, the glorious gardens, and the clean air. It seemed like the perfect place to order her befuddled thoughts, rebuild her fragile confidence, and to come to terms with her marriage to Sonny being over. Her life as she knew it forever changed. This pretty pocket, a quiet oasis in Vermont, was a far cry from the hustle and bustle of central London, but it had all she needed: Town Square Books, and Cobblestone Bakery, whose fudgy brownies, fat, flaky croissants, and fist-sized cinnamon rolls did nothing to help her waistline, The Crooked Porch Cafe for the very best burger in town, and the people here the most welcoming community she had ever been a part of. Verity had no idea when she had arrived that it would be the place. She put down roots and was simply enjoying a holiday with her daughter, Sophie, when fate intervened, wishes came true, and here she was, seven years later!

In truth, it had passed in a blink, another reminder never to take a day for granted.

Darling Sophie, who on that first trip had been no more than a stroppy teen with her phone surgically attached to her palm and was prone to bouts of moodiness when the Wi-Fi was less than speedy. Sophie, who was no longer a teen or stroppy, and was in fact married to Oliver, a chef like her and her dad, Sonny, and expecting her second baby in the autumn. Her darling girl, who Verity doubted now had time to scroll her phone between being mum to Louis and her job as a freelance illustrator. Sophie and her little family lived in

Inverness, Scotland, so very, very far away and a place of equal beauty. How she missed her every day, but not in the way she used to. The pain of separation had certainly eased, plus there was something wonderful about knowing how happy her daughter was, how fulfilled, which meant, as her mum, she worried less. The wonder of FaceTime also meant she got to share a lot of her grandson's life, reading him bedtime stories, and watching him puddle stomp in his red wellingtons. Little Louis, who had quite stolen her heart, and who had Jack wrapped around his chubby, little finger.

Worry was also a luxury she could ill afford with every minute taken up by the farm or the bistro, which was open Tuesday through Saturday for dinner. She and Jack still got precious time together, and she didn't knock herself out to the point of exhaustion as she had when working as a chef before. She had toyed with the idea of changing the name when she became the proprietor but knew as well as anyone that Claudine's had a fantastic reputation, an institution no less.

'Have you tried Claudine's?'

'You must put Claudine's on your list!'

'The crème brûlée at Claudine's is to die for!'

This chatter she overheard while scouring the shelves in *Town Square Books* or queued for her coffee at *The Crooked Porch Cafe.* It helped her understand that the name was entrenched in the community and to change it would not only feel like an act of vandalism but might just be bad for business.

She loved the way the place looked right now in the mid-morning light as she dumped her bag and coat on the vintage hallstand and switched on the lights. Echoes of last night's dinner service still bounced from the walls, the heady infusion of garlic, wine and laughter that was somehow in the walls and furniture. She inhaled the scent of it.

There was something about the cycle of preparing for

service, the ritual of receiving produce from their suppliers, popping the radio on, and singing along (badly) to whatever song lifted her mood. It was a safe and predictable routine that gave structure to her life and was executed with a congenial rhythm in which she found comfort. Gone was the frantic paced nature of working with her ex back in London when the goal had been to grab the attention of the Michelin Guide, harness celebrity endorsements, and to reach and maintain perfection. Many nights in that professional kitchen had been spent pumping coffee into her system just to stop her eyes from closing, as with jittery hands she did her best to maintain the exacting standards where nothing less than the best of the best would do. It had verged on obsession, for Sonny at least, and she had not had the courage nor clarity of thought to rail against it. Like a drunk hamster on a wheel who didn't know how to jump off even if they wanted to.

Running Claudine's as the chef patron was different altogether. Relaxed yet organised mise en place was the key to serving dishes without the added tension in her gut and fear in her bones that it might not pass muster. Not that she didn't hold herself and her food to the very highest of standards, but here the pace suited her, and her brigade was tiny, just her and Debra with a rotation of waiting staff depending on who was available/home from school/needed extra cash/could get a babysitter! It was certainly a community effort and all the better for it.

Debra was Jack's sister and had been resident in Linden Falls for the last couple of years. This beautiful community had welcomed her sister-in-law just as it had her. It wasn't something she had ever shared, but it had been with mixed feelings that she received the news that Jack's sister was relocating here. Selfishly, she had felt the flare of misplaced jealousy at the thought of her time with Jack being diluted. So perfect was their routine, so loving their marriage, the idea of Debra being more present felt like a risk to the lovely harmony of their life, if not their very existence. It was a little mean, she knew, and the delight on Jack's face at the prospect of having his sister closer was enough to buy her silence on the matter.

It was with a shiver of guilt that she now recalled this. How unfounded her concerns! Debra was a wonderful addition to their daily lives and a good friend to her. A sister-in-law who understood boundaries, was kindness itself, who was as independent as she was industrious, motivated, keen to build her own network rather than impose on theirs, and a wonderful cook to boot. She had been helping run Claudine's with reliability and an energy that made all the difference. It had undoubtedly brought the two women closer.

Verity glanced at the clock; Debra would be here any second. A stickler for punctuality, the woman's predictability made her reliable, which again took worry from Verity's shoulders. Shunning the fancy and rather complicated coffee machine, she filled the kettle to make their morning coffee and grabbed their favourite mugs that hung on two hooks – hers said succinctly, *You May Kiss The Cook!* Debra's boasted a lovely hand drawn image of what could have been a person or a planet – it was hard to tell – but it was bright, colourful, and the rather delightful handiwork of Charlotte, the eldest of Debra's two young granddaughters. A knock on the back door drew her from the task.

'Hey, Sol!' Verity smiled at the bearded man who himself looked like a seafarer, and who brought her his daily catch, around which she would design the fish course for the evening.

'Morning, and are you in luck today!'

'Why, what have you got for me?' She watched, eagerly sharing his obvious excitement, as he placed the blue plastic, ice-filled crate on the stainless-steel countertop and plunged his hand into the chilly depths.

'Beautiful brown trout!' He lifted the stunning fish and held it in the air. Its skin glistened and was anything but brown. It was a fine example of this very tasty fish, its skin a golden-tawny colour with a dark back and creamy-yellow belly. Its back and sides carried a stunning pattern of reddish spots.

'Wowsers!' Sol wasn't joking. 'She's a beauty!'

'They all are.' He scooped the ice to reveal a healthy mess of fish.

Instantly, she pictured them with their skin slightly charred, swimming in a garlic/lemon/butter/herb sauce. Her mouth watered at the thought of serving it alongside pomme puree that would be perfectly robust enough to mop up any sauce residue, and a side of fresh asparagus and peas. She'd generously sprinkle the whole thing with fresh parsley and dill, with wedges of lemon on the side.

'Thank you!'

'It's my pleasure as always.' Their friendly fishmonger beamed. 'I have some sea lettuce if you want some? It takes on a stronger umami flavour when dried. I know a couple of my regulars use it as a seasoning or they put it straight into a salad.'

'Ooh, that's a great idea!' She glanced at the clock. 'Debra will know what to do.'

Verity again glanced at the clock. It was unlike her sister-in-law to be late, and she was usually here by now. She'd give her another half an hour and then call. Everyone overslept or faced a mini disaster now and then.

With the lamb racks French trimmed and the herb crust chilling in the fridge, Verity again reached for her phone. Debra was now over an hour and a half late and hadn't responded to her call or her text. It was most unlike her. It was as she was debating hanging up her apron and nipping over to Debra's place that the rear door to the kitchen opened and in walked Jack. It was a wonderful surprise that quite put her sister-in-law's tardiness out of her thoughts.

'Well, this is lovely! Hello, darling. I wasn't expecting—' There was something about his expression that halted the words in her mouth. 'Jack, you don't look well; is everything okay?' She put down the phone and gave her hands a wash before walking over to him.

'No, I …' and then he fell silent as if he'd run out of words. 'I just …'

'You're scaring me,' she whispered. 'Is Sophie okay? The baby? Little Louis?' It was always her nightmare that something terrible might happen and she would not be able to get to her baby girl quickly in her moment of need. It was almost a reflex, the way she put her hand over her heart, as if aware that this was where her hurt would cluster.

'No, no, Sophie's fine, fine. The babies too.'

She exhaled, unaware that she'd been holding her breath. What then? *Truffle? Please, please not her beloved pup … Had they been burgled? A fire? Had he wrecked the car? Was he sick?* Her mind continued to race at a thousand miles an hour.

'I just, erm,' he placed his hands on the countertop as if needing the support of something anchored to the ground. 'I got a call just after you'd left this morning.'

'A call from who?'

'From, from Wyatt who had driven past Deb's place and, ah, he saw an ambulance.'

'An ambulance! Oh my God! Jack, no!' She mentally reached for her car keys, 'What's happened? Did she fall? Is she in the hospital? I'll close up here and we can take one car. What on earth has she done?' She rushed to the stove and turned off the burner, as her husband walked over and held her by the hand. Slowing her down. And she knew … with no more to go on than the set of his mouth, his nonurgent actions, the reluctant, hesitant meeting of her gaze.

'Jack?' She didn't want to say it out loud in case she had

got it wrong; in case her instinct was lying. And how she hoped it was.

'One of her neighbors had called 911. He was out with his dog, walked past and she was on the porch and she'd, she'd gone. Her bag was by her side, door open, like she was heading out and just ...'

'Gone ... *gone*?' She needed it spelled out.

'She's dead. Debra died, honey.'

It was as if the bones were pulled from her very being and she was made soft and at the same time the air was sucked from the room. She stumbled forward and sought out the solidity of the counter, something immovable to hang on to while the whole world seemed to shift.

'I don't believe it, are they *sure*?' Only hindsight would make farcical the question. But in that second of confusion and shock, it was her absolute belief that someone might just have made a mistake, revealing the whole thing to be a ghastly error. Or was it a joke? A terrible, misjudged joke that would allow Debra, her friend, colleague, and sister-in-law to leap from a cupboard to point and laugh. And no matter how distasteful the ruse, Verity would welcome it. She surely would.

Jack's expression, part way between agony and shock, told her there was no mistake and that was when her knees went a little weak.

'I don't know what to do,' she exhaled slowly, and it was as if she did so underwater, the sound of her breathing echoey and loud in her ears. 'Deb should be here by now. We've got ... we've got work to do, fish to prep – and I've made her a coffee.' She stared at the mug with coffee and milk in it – just like she always took it – before bursting into tears.

Jack pulled her into his arms and there they stood, both letting their tears fall as they fought to comprehend the reality of the shocking news.

'Why did she die? What happ … happened?' She hiccupped.

'They need to do some tests and investigate further, but they said it was likely her heart. A heart attack.'

She cried again, as her husband matched her tear for tear.

'Oh Jack, Jack, I'm so sorry! So sorry! It doesn't seem real!' She pulled free from his grip, feeling a little claustrophobic inside his embrace.

'I need to call Shaun …' He wiped his face with his palms.

'Oh God, yes.' It felt awful, knowing how the news was going to floor Debra's son, her only child, and just as bad was the thought of Jack having to deliver it. 'What can I do, my love, what can I do to make it better, to help you?'

'Just stay close, stay close and hold my hand,' her beautiful man implored, as he reached for his phone.

CHAPTER 2

Verity woke on this perfect blue-sky day with a feeling of trepidation lining her gut. It had been this way since they had lost Debra. She felt like she was living in a fragile world that was as scary as it was unnerving. Still in her crumpled linen pyjamas, she threw the bedroom window open and took a moment to appreciate the view: the rolling hills, abundant with elegant clusters of spikey trees, the view down the valley, and – from this vantage point – the beautiful lake in the distance. How she loved this farm, this special, special place. Nearly as much as she loved the man who was at present in the shower, her husband Jack, and the reason she had made Linden Falls her home.

Closing her eyes, she let the winter sunshine glimpse her face, taking in a great lungful of the air that up here on the crest of the farm was like nectar. No longer a Brit abroad, someone wandering through, this place was her home, the people who lived here her community, her friends. She honestly couldn't imagine being anywhere else. And today, more than ever, she needed the love of that community to get her through.

Shaun, and his wife, Arla, had arrived a couple of days ago

to sign paperwork, help organise Debra's affairs and to clear out the rented house. They were all exhausted, pulled brittle by the awful combination of grief and fatigue.

'How you doin'?'

She turned, as Jack came into their bedroom, a wide navy towel around his waist, his hair wet, his body still in the fine shape that physical labour encouraged.

'I'm okay.' She smiled. 'Did you manage to get some rest last night?'

She declined to mention that she'd heard him pacing in the early hours, or the fact his elbow had jabbed her from slumber as he struggled to get comfortable. Nor did she reveal that his heavy sighs of reflection had stopped her nodding off, as she lay on her side and watched the inky dark of night take on the lavender hue of dawn, as day broke. In fact, the best rest she had had was the forty minutes since he had left the bed, no doubt to go and let Truffle out of the back door for her morning visit, and to prep the coffee machine, as he did every morning, and to shower. It was forty minutes she was ridiculously thankful for. It had been a long couple of days.

'Yep.' He nodded. 'Some.'

This was Jack to a tee, not willing to let her in when thoughts troubled him, when worries swirled like mini tornados and his peace was disturbed. He said it was to save her from the concern. She tried to explain that it only meant she worried double, bothered by having to guess at whatever ailed him, and equally disconcerted by his internalization, firmly believing in the old adage that a problem halved …

He had been quiet since his sister's passing and that was, she understood, his prerogative, understanding that there was no one way, nor indeed no *right* way, to do grief.

'It'll all be okay, my love.' She spoke softly, 'It won't be as bad as you're imagining. These things never are.'

He held her eye line.

'If only I shared your optimism. I find that these things are often worse than I have imagined. I just wish I could blink, and the day would be over. I'd like to fast forward the next twelve hours or so.'

'What can I do to make you feel better?' This her way, to find the words of comfort, apply the salve, to love him so much that he might feel the warmth in it and be soothed by it.

'Nothing, Verty.' This his nickname for her, having found the three syllable name at odds with his southern accent when they first met. 'Just be there.'

'You got it.' She smiled and reached for her housecoat; coffee was the first thing on her agenda. 'I love you.'

'I know, and I love you too.'

Jack sat down on the edge of the bed and closed his eyes. She decided to give him the space to gather his thoughts, and not that she would admit it but she too wished she could fast forward the day.

WITH HER HAIR in a loose knot and her dress pressed to perfection, she sat with her eyes to the sky while he drove the winding road to town in silence. Not even the perfect weather or empty roads could tempt them into jollity.

She held his gaze in a slow, lingering look of connection before they climbed from the truck and made their way, hand in hand, towards the chapel.

Now as the beautiful piano music – a pleasant background note of distraction – filled the little church, Jack let go of Verity's hand, squeezing her fingers slightly before he did so, a sign of union, and one from which they both took strength. She sensed he wanted to go forward alone, and understood. It might have been a public occasion, almost, it looked like most of the town was in attendance, yet it was still the burial of his sister. His one chance to say a final goodbye to Debra. And who didn't understand the enormity of such a day, such a moment, one she personally had been dreading and crying over since she was six years of age, when her pup had failed to come home from the vet, and she learned the cruellest lesson that everything living died and that was that.

Images of her dad's funeral filled her mind. It seemed to be this way with grief, that any fresh loss punctured a hole in the skin she had grown to seal away the hurt, letting it all come flooding back to the surface. She cursed her desire to sob, knowing it was not only unseemly, but also that it did her lovely sister-in-law a disservice to allow her passing to be diluted with tears for another.

'Grief is merely the other side of the coin where love is firmly stamped. You can't have one without the other, darling.' Her mother's words offered comfort, even now.

She coughed to clear her throat and watched as Jack walked forward, awkward in the suit and smart shoes that had been consigned to the back of his closet years ago. The trousers now a little loose on the waist and the jacket tight on the arms; farm work will do that to a man.

'You look so nice.' She had watched him grapple with his black tie in the mirror on the wall of their hallway.

'Haven't put this on since Marty's funeral.' Marty, his friend with whom he'd completed three tours of duty. Jack had of course ended up in Linden Falls, where he'd built a life of fishing and painting, before falling in love with her. Marty had not been so lucky, drifting aimlessly from state to state, trying without success to outrun his demons, until the day Jack had ended up buying a good suit in which to see him buried and had cried as they crossed the state line, returning from Marty's flag-draped committal on the saddest of days, gripping her hand like she was an anchor in a storm.

In that moment she was, as ever, thankful for Jack, for their life and their love. Knowing how very different things might have been for them both, had she not come to this pretty town and the universe had not conspired to allow their worlds to collide.

She felt a hand on her arm that pulled her from her thoughts; it was Neva.

'How's he doing?' Neva whispered. The older woman who owned The Wishing Tree Inn, their neighbour and friend for many years, and who now lived in a cottage behind the inn, now run by her niece, Janie, and husband, Max. Neva might not have been as hands on with the business now as she had been, but still very little went on in the inn or, indeed, Linden Falls, without her knowledge.

'As you'd expect.' She took a breath. 'He's sad, shocked. I can't imagine losing my sister.' She pictured the irrepressible Ferne, who lived a life of Labradors, pearls, muddy walks, Sunday roasts plucked from the Aga, and dinner parties in the home counties. The very opposite of her outdoor life here in New England, and one she could not imagine for herself. 'I think when you lose a parent, there's a tiny bit of relief. At least it was like that for me. I wished, of course, that my dad could have gone on forever, but watching him age, part of me was almost waiting for the inevitable, hoping he'd get a good ending and not a crappy one.'

'Well, Amen to that!' Neva nodded.

'But losing a sibling ...' She looked again towards Jack who, with one hand on the casket, and his eyes closed, seemed to be saying his final farewell. It tore at her heart in the way that it did when someone you loved was hurting. 'Especially your only sibling, the only other person in the world who shares the same memories, the same upbringing, the same insight, you even came into being from the same womb. It's a unique bond. I think I'd feel a little adrift if I lost my sister.'

She thought of the hundreds of small, shared private jokes, the one word that could send them into out of control laughter that would mean nothing to anyone else, the songs that placed her on the back seat of her dad's car as they drove the twisty lanes of North Devon on their summer holiday, where she and Ferne would bicker and laugh, and swim in the sea before roasting their shoulders under the warm sun, styling their hair into flicks, thinking it gave them a *Charlie's Angels* type appeal.

'I don't see her that often, but she is my whole childhood. We'd spent hours, as teenagers, trying get our fringes to look like Farrah Fawcett's.'

'That's about the sum of it. It's those small things that bind.' Neva clicked her tongue against the roof of her mouth. 'And by fringe? You mean bangs?'

'You know what I mean.' She shared a smile with the woman. 'It's true though, Neva. When my dad died, it was grim, broke my heart, but also there was this small note of almost joy that it was done. Not only did I not have to dread it anymore, but I got the privilege of saying goodbye to him. I got to watch him sent off. I still miss him, every day,' she looked towards Jack, 'but I guess you never really know how anyone is going to cope. Grief is such a personal thing.'

'It is that. And ain't any of us immune.'

'Where's Henry?' Verity looked towards the door, trying to spot Neva's beau; the two were usually inseparable.

'Chatting out front.' Neva rolled her eyes towards where mourners now gathered.

'Hey, ladies.'

They both turned to see Vera, who had turned down her glam a little and wore a neutral shade of lipstick that wasn't her at all, so used were they to seeing her with her bright mouth and perky smile. Everyone loved Vera, who owned the hair salon just off market square. Vera, who had been married to Wyatt for a few years now, and was so blissfully happy the smile never left her face. Wyatt owned the picture framers in a side street just off the town square; he was a friend of Jack's from way back and the man who had alerted Jack that all was not well when he'd spied the ambulance by Debra's porch.

'Hi, honey.' Neva patted Vera's back.

'I'm going to miss her so much!' Vera pulled a lace-edged hankie from her sleeve and wiped beneath her lashes. 'I remember when she arrived, couple of years ago, and she was just bursting with joy at the thought of being part of this community, excited to be close to Jack and you.' She touched Verity's arm. 'I just thank God that she got to spend her last years in a place she loved and a place that loved her right back.'

'Debra might not have been born and bred here, but it was her home, no doubt about it.' Neva added.

'It really was.' Verity could only agree.

Debra's independence and drive shouldn't have been a surprise; the woman had suffered more than most in her life, a survivor in every sense.

Verity only had the outline of the story, the details too harrowing it seemed for Jack to recount, the timeline sketchy, but she understood that Debra's brute of a husband had been unceremoniously chased from the family home one night. Shaun, their little boy, had been in the house and had heard the whole thing. Shaun, who now sat at the front of this very chapel, while Arla, his diminutive wife, gripped his hand.

Debra, the pretty woman who baked apple pies and placed them on a gingham tablecloth for her family, who laundered their clothes, cut flowers from the garden, and arranged them into vases, who smiled at her neighbours, organised carpool for school, and opened her home for Thanksgiving celebrations, and held birthday parties in the yard … Debra, who was also the victim of domestic abuse. It was just unthinkable.

Verity knew that on the fateful night when everything

had changed Debra had simply bolted the door behind her husband and got on with her life, raising a strong boy and working hard in the process. This, only one reason among many, that Verity so admired her sister-in-law, and only one of the reasons she would so miss her. Debra always said, and Verity could not disagree, that the one benefit of having a lousy father who was a worse husband, was that it showed her son how not to do it, and Shaun was indeed the gentlest and very best of young men. He and Arla were smitten, their two young daughters, Charlotte and Eva, who had been left in the care of Arla's parents back in Portland, a delight.

With the congregation now seated and a respectful hush of anticipation from all gathered, Jack patted Shaun's shoulder and, on his cue, stood and took a solemn walk to the lectern. She watched, as her husband, who had practised his eulogy relentlessly, stood quietly, taking a moment, as he gripped the wooden stand with both hands. Briefly he caught her eye, no doubt to help steady his nerves, as he drew breath and began to speak.

'That we are here at all is such a shock to me, to us all. That said, it's heartening to see so many people here today to celebrate and give thanks for the life of Debra May Darby. We are truly grateful for your attendance and for your love at this time, which we have felt in abundance, and, trust me when I tell you, it has made all the difference. Deb was mother to Shaun. Gammy to Charlotte and Eva, mother-in-law to Arla. She was my little sister and a friend to all of you. In fact, a friend to anybody who needed one. That was her nature, her kindness, her instinct. Everyone loved her. She would, of course, be mortified by the fuss we're all making, and also, I'm sure, delighted by the sight of the flowers. She always loved flowers and even when,' he paused and swallowed. Verity resisted the temptation to jump up and go stand next to him, wanting in that moment to wrap her arms around him and hold him close. 'Even when things were tough for her, the times in her life that were less than happy, she always found time to tend to the garden, cut her beloved blooms and display them all over the house.' He took a moment to gather himself, to compose his thoughts. 'As most of you know, Deb only came to Linden Falls a few years back, and I consider myself very lucky that I was able to spend that time with her, laughing with her, walking with her, and letting her cheat at cards which, let me tell you, for a churchgoing, God fearing woman, she did with a poker face that I still couldn't call!' A ripple of laughter made its way around the room. 'We, her family, would like to thank …'

Jack drew breath to continue, but halted, as the door at the rear of the chapel opened and some, with suitable stares of admonishment, turned to see who the latecomer was. Others kept their eyes to the front, trying not to let Jack get thrown off his stride. She stared at her husband, his eyes were fixed on that door and the interloper. His mouth fell open a little and his face turned a particular shade of grey. It was at the sight of this that she too turned and watched a man of average build and average height remove his hat, folding it into his chest, over his heart, before taking a seat at the back of the room.

Jack looked up, coughed, and blinked, concentrating once again on the text in front of him. 'We would like to thank all of you who have written to us, called, or arrived at the farm, to share your stories of the difference Deb made in your lives and the lives of our community. And, boy, has she been busy!' Again, that ripple of laughter. 'When she wasn't laughing alongside Verty at the bistro, she worked within this very church, feeding the needy, helping kids learn to read at the school, even knitting hats and scarves to send to those on the streets or who have hit a hard time, stave off the cold.' He took a beat, 'I don't know if there is such a thing, but she had the very best kind of passing. No long illness or undue suffering, Deb simply blinked, and her time was done,' his voice cracked. Verity watched as Arla placed her arm around Shaun's heaving shoulders. Jack turned towards the blonde wood coffin where the stunning arrangement of lilies nestled on the top. Phil, who owned Bertie's Petals, the favoured florist in town, had done a truly fine job with the displays. 'Linden Falls will miss you, Sis. Shaun and Arla, your girls, Verty, and I, we will all miss you, more than we can say. God speed.'

The choir took their positions, and their voices rang out loud as their sweet harmonies floated up through the rafters. Verity was no believer; yet, in that moment, even she was sure this celestial music of praise might just travel all the way up to Heaven itself.

CHAPTER 3

The service, everyone agreed, was faultless. Jack and Shaun, in particular, received the warm hugs and handshakes of those wanting to help ease the pain of their loss. Pam Olson, who as her personal trainer had helped whip Debra into shape and become a friend, read a beautiful poem that left not a dry eye in the house. It was as they travelled home to White Cedar Farm that Verity lay her hand on Jack's thigh,

'You did a great job, my darling.'

'I hope so.'

'Oh, you really did. I'm proud of you. My turn now.' She pulled a face, hoping the buffet would honour her sister-in-law and that the wake would go off without a hitch.

There had been much debate over whether to hold her wake at Claudine's or at the farm, all agreeing that the homely environment of the farm would be more fitting. The truth was, Verity had not set foot in the bistro since Debra's passing. A notice had been tacked up on the door, on the rare chance there was someone local who had not heard their sad news, and for the benefit of tourists explaining their temporary closure. Not that she could afford to remain closed much longer, not with bills to pay and a loan to service. But the thought of prepping for service, the radio playing, her mug sitting forlornly on the shelf, life carrying on without Debra, it wasn't something she relished.

'I can't believe it, Verty.' Jack shook his head.

'I know, it's a lot; it's realisation, it's finality, but I guess that's the point of a funeral,'

'No,' he cut her short, 'I'm talking about the guy that came in after I'd started, who stood at the back, scampering in like a rat from the back of a dumpster, trying to stay in the shadows!' He gripped the steering wheel, his knuckles turning white. It wasn't like him, not at all. Her placid man, who had worked through so much in his own journey, right now sat beside her like a coiled spring.

'Who is he?' Verity knew she hadn't seen him before.

'It's him. Todd Miller. Shaun's dad. Deb's ex-husband,' he spat.

'Oh! Well, that's a turn up for the books.'

She had heard nothing but dire tales of his violent behaviour and his adultery. The kind of man she disliked before they had exchanged a single word, based on the fact that tales of his exploits came from mouths she did trust, Jack and Shaun, primarily. Debra never mentioned him or her marriage, and this too she more than understood. Sometimes it was easier to leave wounds to heal.

'Yep. He's got some nerve coming here. What in God's name did he think? That we'd invite him for a drink and a catch up on old times before sending him on his way? Or maybe he brought a casserole?' He clenched his jaw – even with this flippant remark.

'Death brings out different reactions in different people, maybe.'

'No, no, no,' he shook his head again, 'no, honey, this guy

doesn't get a hall pass, there's no handshake of forgiveness, nothing like that for him, never!'

It was rare to see Jack so animated, so angry. He breathed heavily.

'I understand, my love, I do—'

'You don't, Verty, you can't! Shaun was there in the house that night, just a little kid. In his room along the hallway with his night light glowing and his football posters on the wall. That house should have been his haven. It should have been Deb's haven too, her *home*! Shaun never got over it, how could he? That POS beat on his Ma!' He banged the steering wheel. 'I swear if I'd gotten hold of him ...'

Verity stayed silent, letting him vent, understanding how grief was often tinged with equal parts anger and regret, and hoping he might get it out of his system before they arrived home to welcome their guests to Debra's wake.

'I tell you, now, he better be on the first stage out of Dodge because, if I see his face, I will do to him what he did to my sister! I'll show him how it feels to be scared!'

'Actually, Jack, you're kind of scaring *me*!' It was a phrase that was alien between them and shocking that her kind, kind man could elicit this at all.

His expression changed and his shoulders seemed to lose some of their tension, as his grip on the steering wheel lessened.

'I'm just angry.'

'I know. I know, my love.'

'It's a lot is all. Him turning up on top of me having to say goodbye to my sister. How *dare* he?'

'Did Shaun see him, do you think?' Her fear was that, with the young man coping with the loss of his mother, throwing his estranged father into the mix could not lead to anything good.

'I'm not sure. By the time we left the chapel Todd had

gone, but whether Shaun saw his dad outside, I don't know. It's the last thing the boy needs.'

She thought it most telling how Jack still thought of Shaun as 'the boy,' even though he was himself a father of two. Not that she had any right to judge him on that, knowing how she had to fight the urge to give Sophie advice as if she were a child too.

He pulled the truck in front of the barn and killed the ignition.

'You go in, honey. I just need a minute,' he whispered.

'Take all the time you want.' Leaning over, she kissed him gently on the cheek. 'I can welcome everyone. Do what you need to, go for a walk or disappear to the lake or—'

'It's okay, I'll sit here, clear my head, and then I'll be right in.' Reaching for her hand he raised it to his lips and kissed her fingers. 'Thank you, Verty.'

'What for?' She ran her hand over the side of his face, torn to see him hurting and knowing there was so very little she could do to fix it.

'For being there. For loving me.'

'That's a given.' A car drove past them along the track, heading towards the farmhouse. 'I'd better go.'

With the creases smoothed from the front of her frock, and wispy tendrils of her hair that had worked loose tucked behind her ears, Verity wedged the front door open and busied herself in the kitchen, pulling platters of food from the fridge, the pickles from the larder, and the freshly baked rolls that she'd left cooling on a wire rack she piled into a napkin-lined basket. The cakes she took from their tins and placed it all onto the dining table of their spacious, open-plan home.

'It was a lovely service.' Vera spoke, as she leant a hand, removing the Saran Wrap from the potato salad and the charcuterie board that Verity had lovingly prepared.

'It really was.' She counted the plates under her breath and hoped she had put enough out.

'How's that husband of yours doing? Wyatt said Jack didn't want to talk to him about Deb, didn't want to talk about much.' This Vera whispered; seemingly she too had picked up on his rather fraught aura that was as unlike him as it was unnerving.

'It's a lot, a big day,' she offered the mealy-mouthed catch-all, 'he's tired, we all are. He'll be fine. I've left him in the truck. He just needs a minute.' She looked out over the front yard, hoping to see his face.

'Well, you know where I am.' Vera held her gaze with a knowing look; it was always this way, her friend reassuring Verity that no matter what, she was there for her. 'Wyatt too, if Jack ever does want to talk or go fishing.'

'Not that Jack needs an excuse to go fishing!'

'Wyatt too. I'm glad they're friends.'

'Me too.' She spoke as Shaun walked in with Arla. 'Hey, you two, we were just saying what a wonderful service it was.'

Shaun nodded and gripped his wife's hand like she was driftwood, and he was all at sea.

'I've been dreading it and yet it felt like it lasted seconds.'

'I know,' she remembered this feeling from her dad's funeral, 'please eat something, Shaun, I'll worry less about you if you eat something.'

'I'll go get you a plate.' Arla headed towards the table as Jack finally came in.

'So, I guess, Verty has told you?'

She shook her head as subtly as she was able.

'Told me what?' Shaun asked calmly.

Jack walked forward and placed his arm on his nephew's shoulder, saying, 'Todd was in the chapel. Your dad.'

Shaun snorted his derision and placed his hands on his hips.

'Are you *kidding* me?'

'Nope.' Jack enunciated.

'Why would he turn up?' Shaun sighed.

'Search me.' Jack pulled a face, his jaw tight.

'Well, as far as I'm concerned, he ain't my dad. He forfeited that right the night he walked out!'

'Oh, I hear ya.' Jack offered his support, raising his palms to show his lack of protest.

'I don't know what I'd do if I saw him.' Shaun looked towards the door as if wondering this for the first time, and simultaneously half-expecting him to walk in.

'You don't have to worry, Shaun,' Jack stood firm, 'I won't let him near you.'

'It's strange,' Shaun took a beat. 'Part of me *wants* to see him, wants to tell him what I think of him. I imagine that confrontation sometimes, I always have. I don't know why; I guess there are things that are left unsaid between us, questions I have for him.'

'I have one or two myself.' Jack flexed his knuckles.

'Especially since I became a dad. I can't imagine not seeing Charlotte or Eva, just not seeing them! Staying away, by choice. It blows my mind. And yet that's what he did, just walked out of my life ...'

She hated the sorrow in Shaun's tone, the echo of rejection.

'I was only a little kid, last time I saw him. That night, it's etched in my brain.'

'Deb was mother enough and father enough to you,' Jack whispered.

'She was. She really was.' Shaun swiped at the tears that gathered. Arla returned with two plates, laden with food.

'Come on, Shauny, let's go find a quiet corner and eat!'

Verity smiled at the young woman, who might have been bird-like in stature, but was a warrior when it came to looking after her man. Verity loved her for it.

'Hey,' Jack called in greeting as Neva and Henry arrived.

'A beautiful service.' Neva squeezed Jack's arm.

'And we've been to a few! At our age it's hard not to.' Henry pointed towards the couch, as if spying the place he intended to sit.

She and Jack shared a small smile, both thankful for Henry and the lightning of the mood.

'I've been to more than I would have liked too,' Jack spoke openly, and Henry nodded. 'It could have been a double committal today if I'd got my hands on one of the congregation.'

'Oh?' This had caught Neva's attention.

'The man who came in late, and then crept out before we all gathered at the front, that was Debra's ex-husband, Shaun's father. Not seen hide nor hair of him for decades and then he had the gall to pitch up today.'

Neva sighed; she clearly knew Debra's story.

'I guess he had his reasons for turning up.' The woman offered her wisdom.

'None I want to hear!' Jack was unflinching.

'Please, Neva, Henry, go and eat some food!' She was keen to change the subject, not wanting her sister-in-law's wake to be dominated by talk of Todd Miller. She shot Jack a look, reminding him that this was neither the time nor the place.

If the funeral had passed in a flash, the same could not be said of the wake, where folks seemed happy to linger. And why not? There was plenty of food and drink, the music was low, and it was nice to catch up with neighbours and friends on this sun-filled day.

It was with relief that Verity, with the beginnings of headache, finally closed the front door, having waved good night to the Olsons, and then Jed Duncan and his family who ran the hardware store. She kicked off her shoes, and let her bare feet cool against the wooden floor, before sinking down into the chair by the window. The wake had gone off without a hitch. The food was well received and, as ever, the chef in Verity took joy from the empty bowls and clean plates that were stacked and awaiting her attention on the countertop. Copious quantities of tea had been drunk and even the odd bottle or two of wine.

Jack came down the stairs in his running gear.

'Thought I'd hit the trail, go up around the loop and back again, try and clear my head. I'll take Truffle; she needs to burn off some of those treats people have been sneaking her today.'

'You go for a run, my love,' It was a relief to see him calmer, 'but can you leave Truffle? I want the company. I'm going to sit here and do precisely nothing.'

'Sure.'

She watched him walk to the door,

'Do you think,' he began.

'Do I think what?' she sat up a little straighter.

'Do you think I should have confronted Todd? Did I let Deb down?'

'No, no, my love. First, you could never and did never let her down. You were always there for her, and she loved you very much. Second, how would that have panned out? You confronting him in the chapel? If you'd made a scene or made Shaun feel uncomfortable then that would have been letting her down. You did exactly right, you made sure it was all about her and that she was honoured.'

'Maybe.' He didn't sound convinced.

'See you in a bit,' Jack called back to Verity as he ventured out into the cooling air of dusk.

Verity tipped her head back in the chair and closed her eyes, enjoying the moment of solitude among the chaos of the last few days: the shock of losing Debra, trying to help Jack with his grief while managing her own, planning for the funeral, feeling the dreadful pull of pressure that the bistro had remained closed … She was tired and welcomed the idea of drifting off for a minute or two. Her phone buzzed on the end table.

'What is it they say? No rest for the wicked?' she spoke into the ether and ran her hand over her face, before jumping up to grab her phone. It was Neva calling.

'Hi Neva, all okay?' It was her nature to be concerned; the woman wasn't getting any younger and Henry was looking a little physically frail, she had thought, despite his charm and that twinkle in his eye.

'Yep, just wanted to, erm,' the woman's hesitancy was out of character. Neva, also known as the "keeper of wishes," was the person who pulled down the wishes tied to the branches of the big old Linden Falls tree that folklore said made them come true. She then catalogued them in her precious book and was never usually hesitant when it came to speaking her mind.

'What is it?' she asked softly. 'Has something happened?'

'No, no, I just thought I should call because—'

'Neva, you're scaring me!' This the second time she had said this in recent times. It didn't feel good.

'The man Jack was talking about, Debra's ex.'

'Yes, Todd. What about him?'

'He's checked into the inn. Knowing what I know, I'd have probably put out the "No Vacancies" sign, but Janie was on reception and, well, he's paid in advance for three nights.'

'Three nights?' Verity rubbed her eyes; this was all she needed. 'Thank you for letting me know, Neva. And it's no one's fault, not yours, not Janie's, the man is after all entitled to book a room wherever he wants. I just wish it was anywhere other than here. Speak soon, Neva.'

'Good night, dear.'

With her peace now disturbed, Verity sat back, as Truffle lay on her feet. Their beautiful girl always seemed to sense when she was in need of contact.

'Two questions, Truff. Why would Todd Miller need to

hang around for three nights, and, more importantly, how do I keep this fact from your daddy?'

Truffle seemed to sigh in a way that was almost human and gave Verity a much needed laugh on this the trickiest of days.

CHAPTER 4

After his run, and as night pulled its blind on the day, Jack took his time having his second shower. Truffle had managed to worm her way upstairs and now lay on their patchwork comforter at the foot of their bed. They did this sometimes, let her cuddle up while they read or watched a movie, before they lured her downstairs to make her night-time visit and covertly rewarded her with a bedtime, bone-shaped biscuit; the fact that they both did this, while swearing their dog to secrecy, was only funnier when they both confessed. She was a spoiled and much-loved pup, no doubt.

'How was your run?' Verity asked as she worked her night cream into the skin of her neck and face.

'Good.' His succinct reply.

In his plaid pyjama bottoms and white T-shirt, with his hair damp, he sat down hard on his side of the bed and plugged his phone in to charge. It made her smile. He might no longer be a military man, but the precision and methodical way in which he executed his nighttime routine was clearly a hard habit to break. His phone was then turned face down onto his bedside cabinet. He neatly folded the strap of his watch behind the face and lay that next to his phone for easy reach in the night. The glass of water was on its coaster and set in front of the lamp and his top pillow was removed and placed on the deep window seat. Her side of the bed, in contrast, was chaotic with her pillows haphazardly piled and punched into place. She slept with one leg dangling from the mattress and there were a pile of books waiting to be read on her nightstand. On top of the books, she had balanced a box of tissues, a bottle of makeup remover, a nail file, a little enamel tray for jewellery, a photograph of Sophie and Louis and, quite inexplicably, a half empty packet of peanut M&M's.

She always thought anyone looking at no more than their bed could gauge so much about their characters. Jack climbed beneath the duvet and Truffle shifted to accommodate his feet, giving him a dirty look to have been so inconvenienced.

'Five minutes, Truff, and then you are heading downstairs,' he spoke softly to his girl.

'Well, we did it, Jack, we got through today and it was wonderful really, lovely to hear people speak about Deb so fondly.'

'It was.'

'I hope Shaun sleeps well; they're coming over for breakfast tomorrow. It'll be good to see him and Arla before they head back to Portland.'

'Yep. One thing for sure, I'm going to sleep a whole lot better knowing Todd's outta here. His presence in that chapel has bothered me.' He sighed loudly and her heart flipped. It didn't feel good, having a secret from him, knowledge that she knew would unsettle him further when all she wanted for him was peace. 'I didn't think for one minute he might turn up here. The only consolation I can take is that Deb ain't never going to have another funeral and I won't ever see the sorry excuse of a man again.'

'Mmmnn.' She nodded, wishing Neva hadn't called, wishing she didn't know that the man was in fact only a couple of miles away, sleeping under the roof of the inn.

Jack turned slowly to face her.

'Why is there something about your reply that unnerves me?'

She shook her head, 'I don't know.'

'Verty, I know you well enough to know what your silence or little noises mean. We both know you're a terrible liar and, when there's a risk of you being found out, you go quiet, I mean, let's face it, you are rarely quiet or without something to say!'

He smiled at her, and she laughed, softly. This was true.

'And so, the question is, wife of mine,' he shifted onto his side and rested his head on his hand, propped up by his elbow, 'what aren't you telling me?'

'Don't be mad,' she began; her mouth felt sticky with nerves.

'Don't be mad? Those words make me *feel* mad! It's like telling someone to calm down or don't think of a blue goat!'

'Now I'm thinking of a blue goat.' She pictured this very thing.

'Exactly!' He sighed.

'Okay,' she scootched into a seated position, resting against her pillows, knowing this was not going to be best delivered if she was already three quarters of the way to sleep, 'Neva called,' she paused.

'Uh-huh.' It was as if he was urging her to get to the point, something she was trying to avoid.

'She thinks that Todd might be staying at the inn.'

'Sonofa ...' he took a deep breath. 'She *thinks*? Surely she knows if he is or isn't. She must be aware if he has checked in or not, if he's staying in *her* inn or somewhere else entirely.'

In other circumstances, she'd have wrinkled up her nose and pointed out that it was the only inn in Linden Falls, but this was not other circumstances and there was no room for sarcasm or humour. They were talking about Todd Miller, the man who had hurt Debra and who had walked out on his son without a second glance. The man who had got under Jack's skin.

'All right, Jack! She *knows* he is staying there. She knows this.'

'Are you kidding me right now?' He raised his voice. She said nothing, understanding the rhetorical nature of his question.

Jack threw back the duvet and leapt from the warmth of their bed, before opening his closet door, pulling a sweatshirt over his T-shirt, and grabbing his jeans from the hanger.

'Where are you going?' Her heart raced. This was the last thing she wanted and the last thing her husband needed: to be heading into town with anger pulsing in his veins.

'I'll give you three guesses!'

'I really don't think it's a good idea, love!' She raised her voice so her urgent tone matched his rather frantic actions.

He either didn't hear, was in no mood to listen or couldn't give a flying fig about her views on the matter. She heard his hurried footsteps on the wooden stairs and, with all thoughts of sleep now fled, her body jumpy with tension, she sprang from her bed and followed him. Jack grabbed his boots from the rack by the door and put them on; next he took his car keys from the hook.

With his hand grabbing the door handle, she implored him, 'Jack, please just wait a second! You need to calm down! I mean, what's the plan? To go and throw stones at every window of the inn until Todd pops his head out? Then what? Ask him to come down so you can punch him in the face? Please think about it! It's late. It's been the hardest of days for us all, and for it to end with you spending a night in the county jail on an assault charge would not be a fitting tribute to your sister! It would be all anyone would talk about, all they'd remember, and that is not fair on Debra. Not fair on any of us.'

His head fell forward, and he let go of the handle. She walked forward and wrapped her arms around his waist. Laying her head on his back, she spoke softly.

'I love you, Jack Darby. I love your passion, I love your defence of your family. But the anger you feel towards that man is wrapped in your grief and you need to try and separate the two. There is no benefit in getting yourself in trouble to settle a score or avenge what happened. Life doesn't work that way, no matter how often we wish it did.'

He shrugged free of her grasp and walked to the kitchen where the moonlight cast its silvery shards of magic over the slate floor.

'You can't judge me; you don't get a say!' Anger guided his words and she let them coast from his mouth, knowing he was good and kind and fair, and that this outburst would haunt him later, but they'd recover, of course they would. 'That night,' he paused and took a deep breath; his chest heaved with the effort of all it tried to contain. 'That night when Shaun called me I'll never forget. My number was pinned to the phone in case of an emergency. He was only a little kid, and he was scared, and Deb was locked in her room, and I was miles away, on exercise, and I couldn't get to them. I couldn't make it better!' His voice cracked.

'But Jack, you wouldn't have been able to make it better even if you'd been next door! I don't know much about what happened, but I'm willing to bet that that night was the result of a cumulation of events, the finale to a whole string of rows or whatever that had been building until they reached boiling point. It nearly always is. It's rarely one isolated event, but more often it's something that lights the touchpaper that's been present for some time. Not that it makes it any easier to swallow, but the fact is, it happened and it's terrible, truly terrible, but it's not your fault!'

'No, it's *his* fault and right now I know where he's hiding out!' He paced.

'Have you asked yourself why he is checked in for three nights, what possible reason he might have to stay here?'

'Three nights?' He stopped pacing. 'He's here in my town for *three* nights?'

She let the fact slip, forgetting momentarily that she hadn't shared this with her husband.

'So, what happens now, then, Verty, what do you want? You expect me to stay out of his way? Give him free rein in Linden Falls, in *my* hometown? Let him go get lunch at The Crooked Porch? Chat to Nicole? Or maybe he can sit with Henry in the town square and talk about the weather? God, the man has got some nerve! I cannot sit back and let him wander around the place Debra loved, the place where she was free of him, a place she spent her final years without the shadow of him over her life? How would that be fair?'

'If it's fairness you want, Jack, then you might be a long time waiting.' She folded her arms across her chest. 'Nothing about this is fair. And to answer your questions, what I want is for us to try and get some sleep so that tomorrow is marginally less difficult than today, and what I *expect* is you to consider that it is not only about you and how you feel. It's about Shaun, about me, about Neva too. How would that be for her if you went to the inn and caused a ruckus?'

Finally, he put his car keys on the countertop and leaned against the sink as he slipped off his boots.

'I've never felt this way before,' he whispered into the half light of the kitchen, 'never felt so angry, and so helpless.'

'It's grief, my love. Fully loaded grief.'

'It was different when Mom and Dad died.' He looked up at her, his expression one that tore at her heart, a man who wanted the answers she was unable to give.

'Yes. You've lost your sister. It's all new and all shit.'

'It really is.'

'Come on, let's go back to bed.'

Verity reached for his hand and guided him up the stairs to their room. They both stood in the doorway and welcomed the laughter that was a visceral reaction to the sight that greeted them. Truffle was no longer on their comforter but had wiggled under the duvet and, with her big head on one of Verity's pillows, was sprawled in the middle of the bed, snoring loudly with her head tipped back, eyes closed, in a deep slumber that Verity could only envy.

'I'll shift her,' Verity took charge.

'No,' Jack placed his hand on her arm, her sweet, sweet man. 'She looks so comfortable, let her have five minutes ...'

WITH BACON CRISPING under the grill, glossy eggs sizzling in the pan, and thick slices of French toast in the warming oven, Verity poured fresh orange juice into tall glasses and took them to the table. She had gone to a lot of trouble, wanting Shaun and Arla to have a decent breakfast before they headed off. Fresh flowers picked from the garden for yesterday's buffet were cut shorter and placed in jam jars that she dotted around the immaculately pressed, white tablecloth. Linen napkins graced the crackle-glazed plates with their scalloped edges, and ketchup was decanted into a mini tureen, and the maple syrup was in her great grandmother's milk jug. She was looking forward to eating. Her appetite had been a little off since Debra's passing, but today she felt the stir of want in her stomach and was glad of it.

Later she would go to the bistro, clean up, and get ready for opening the day after tomorrow when she'd had a chance to order produce and plan her menu. It was, she knew, the right thing to do, to carry on with her life and spend time in the place that she and Debra had loved working in together. But, my goodness, she was not looking forward to it. It would be so odd not having her sister-in-law by her side.

Sadly, the loan repayments paid little heed to her grief or her feelings of loss. She had no choice other than to pull up her big girl pants and get her hands dirty.

Jack and Truffle were in the yard, and through the window came the melodic chirp of birdsong. It was some relief to her that they had both slept solidly for eight hours, unsure what the mood might have been today if they had to handle it with fatigue rattling their bones.

'Look who I found?' Jack was full of bonhomie, that she knew was a mask, as he did his best to make this a good day for Shaun and Arla too. She was beyond happy that they were on the same page for that at least.

'How was the lodge? Cozy enough?' She greeted Arla with a kiss on the cheek.

The lodge was the guest accommodation where family and friends stayed. Sophie, Oliver, and Louis its most regular guests. She and Jack had renovated it a couple of years back. While retaining the wooden features and rustic feel of the old log cabin, she had added a luxurious mattress to the old iron bedstead and had updated the soft furnishings with fancy Roman blinds and matching cushions in a stunning French ticking. With the prettiest white, Egyptian cotton bedding she could afford, the plumbing overhauled, a powerful rain shower and underfloor heating, staying there was a joy.

'I could quite happily stay there forever.' Arla smiled. 'It's so peaceful.'

'Although the kids might miss us,' Shaun reminded her playfully.

'What garbage! They're with my parents. They'll be eating candy before bedtime, dancing barefoot in the garden, collecting bug-infested twigs and rocks from the forest and will be able to snub their vegetables and demand ice cream without fear of anyone making them eat a carrot first! They are having the best time!'

'All very good points,' Shaun had to concede. 'I just wanted to say thank you, Verity, for everything you did yesterday. You too, Jack.'

'That's what family is for.' Jack reminded him, gripping the young man's shoulder, as they all gravitated towards the dining table. Their stomachs too, it seemed, in sync with hers.

Verity ferried the food from the kitchen and was delighted to see everyone tucking in heartily. A welcome hiatus from the pull of grief. It was what she did – fed people – and to hear their lip smacks of delight and to watch them greedily scoop what she had prepared into their mouths was all the thanks she needed.

'I kind of didn't want to raise the topic, Shaun, but I think you should know that Todd is still in town. I didn't want you driving past him or hearing it from someone else.'

'How do you know he's still in town?' Shaun placed his cutlery on his empty plate and finished his mouthful.

'He checked into the inn. Neva called last night to let us know.' Jack filled in the detail.

'Maybe he's already gone, made an early start.' Shaun reasoned.

She and Jack looked at each other across the table, both aware there was no early start for Todd who was set to stay for another couple of nights.

'Maybe.' She sipped her coffee, avoiding Shaun's eye line.

'It stirred up some silt knowing he was around, I can tell you.' Shaun leant his elbows on the table. 'I dreamt about him, which I haven't done for years, dreamt about that night.'

Arla put her hand on her husband's leg, the contact, Verity was sure, of great comfort.

'It was the first time he's spoken about it so openly to me.' Arla looked saddened, yet simultaneously proud. 'And I think that's a really positive thing.'

'I think you're right.' She winked at the woman who clearly loved Shaun.

'We spoke about it too.' Jack spoke up, 'I tried to explain to Verty how I will always feel guilty about not being closer, about not being there to protect you and your mom.'

Shaun nodded and let his head hang forward a little.

'It's still strange to me how my whole life could be ripped apart in such a short time. I thought my parents were happy, I thought I was happy, but it wasn't real, none of it, and that makes me feel so dumb. Even though I was only a kid, I kinda grew up that night.'

'I hate that you had to.' Jack interjected.

'I know, Jack. I know. And you have always been there for me and Mom. But it changed everything for me. When I look back over my life, it's a marker, a wound. There was my life before that night and then my life after. I remember it felt like there was something in the air, forewarning some might say. Or maybe that's only how I look back at it. But I could tell something was off, I knew something was brewing. Like that feeling you have before a bad storm when you can't yet see the rain or hear the thunder, but you know it's a comin'. It was like that.' Shaun took a beat and composed himself. It was as if he had the need to talk and they were more than willing to listen. 'The old man got in from work, had had a couple of beers in front of the TV which wasn't that unusual. I think he ate his supper in his chair. I'd checked my baseball cards, had them all laid out on the table, then I went up to bed and read a little, and I must have fallen asleep but the light on my nightstand was still on and I was woken up by the sound of a crash, a bang, something falling or being pushed, who knows, but her voice yelling and him, silent. I couldn't make out what she was saying but I've guessed at it many times, tried to make her frightened yelling into something tangible; my mind replays it, *"get off me!" "Don't hurt me!" "You'll wake Shaun!"* I know I heard my name, and then, *"Please, no! Stop it! I'm sorry ..."* or possibly a combination of all of them. I'll never know for sure because I never found the courage to ask her. Thought it was too painful to bring up. But what I heard ....' He looked skyward and blinked away the tears that gathered in his eyes, this young man who didn't cry easily. 'There was glass smashed, furniture hurled, the odd shout, whimpering and then tears leaching from beneath the gap in the bedroom door. There was blood too, liquid sorrow that stained the patterned rug that ran up the middle of the corridor. And no matter how many years passed or each birthday or Christmas that we celebrated without him sitting at our table, I only had to put a foot on that rug and I saw it and I felt it, the echo of that night, lurking like a bad smell – and the sounds, there for perfect recall whenever I needed them. I wish they weren't.'

'I'm so sorry, Shaun.' She spoke the only words she could, knowing there was no platitude that could bring healing.

'Me too. I'm sorry for Mom, sorry we had to live that way, sorry that even now, after her passing, it's still like a thorn in my skin. It's even put a slice of discord between you and I.' He stared at Arla.

'Nothing can do that, baby.' The sweet woman reached out and ran her hand over his scalp.

'But it does! When I close down or clam up or when we have to discipline the kids and I'm so scared of turning out like him that I am almost paralysed with fear!'

'You are the best daddy those girls could have, the very best, never doubt it! I just wish I could understand how to support you better. More than that I wish I could take away your hurt.' Arla spoke from the heart.

'I love you, Arla.'

'And I you.' She smiled at him.

'I never want to be like him!'

'You are *not* like him.' Arla spoke decisively, holding his eye line as if this might help the words sink in. 'You are not like him at all.'

'Well, I'll never know, will I? I don't even know where he lives or what he does, and he knows zip about me.'

'He's here for another couple of days.' She spoke without too much forethought, 'He checked in for three nights, so, yes, another couple of days.'

Verity stared at her husband whose mouth moved, but it seemed he couldn't find the words.

'Maybe we should stay a bit longer?' Arla spoke quietly, addressing Shaun, as if she too understood that his was his decision, and what he wanted that mattered.

'Maybe we should.' He held his wife's gaze, which only highlighted to Verity how Jack now avoided hers.

CHAPTER 5

It was settled. Shaun and Arla had spoken to Charlotte and Eva who were more than happy to stay an extra night or two with their grandparents. Arla's prediction was right; it seemed they were having the best time. No sooner had Verity waved the young couple off down the track when Jack again stood with his hands on his hips. This, she was learning, his preferred stance for an argument.

'Well, that was interesting.' His tone was clipped.

'Interesting? I was going to say successful; I think the food went down well and it was nice being just the four of us.' She spoke as she cleared the table and started stacking the dirty plates into the dishwasher. Avoidance at its best as she felt entirely without the energy for another fight.

'You know what I mean,' he countered.

'I do, Jack, but, in all honesty, I am in no mood to have you shout or go cold or tell me how I've messed up. You're not the only one going through this, and God knows I am trying to be there for you, but feeling like I'm walking on eggshells is doing me no favours at all! It's bloody exhausting.'

'Did you hear what Shaun said about that night?'

'Yes, I heard it, and it was dreadful, absolutely dreadful!' She knew his words – and how her heart ached for him and Debra – would stay with her.

'And yet you still thought it okay to tell Shaun to stick around for, what, a great reunion?'

'I did not tell Shaun to stick around! That was Arla's idea!' She hated the indignation of being falsely accused.

'Do you know the worst thing about this, Verty?'

Yes, the fact that you and I are on different sides of the fence, shouting and hollering at each other as if we are any other couple! And we are not and never have been any other couple, Jack! We are golden, we are wonderful, we are about as perfect together as it gets, and this is awful, just awful! This she kept to herself.

'It's that we should be mourning Deb! We should be concentrating on the loss of her, but instead Todd has hijacked that! It's become all about Todd! About him hanging around and us guessing at his motives!'

'It isn't, Jack, it's not about that at all! That's only how *you* feel. It's actually about us as a family trying to figure out where we all go from here—'

'Well, it seems that you already have it all figured out—'

'What exactly do you mean by that?' Her voice had gone up an octave.

'It means you think we should all forgive and forget and give Todd a second chance and, hey, why not invite him over for dinner? Fancy telling Shaun that he was sticking around!'

'First, Jack, you have gone from zero to one hundred very quickly and are quite mistaken. I have said no such thing! Don't you dare use me as your sparring partner just because you are wound up and angry! Don't you dare take it out on me! Why would you *not* tell Shaun? Why would you think he doesn't have the right to know? He's not that scared kid in his bedroom anymore, he's a grown-ass man. And second, don't ever presume to know what I am thinking or feeling, as that, my love, is the road to disaster! *Never* judge me or make decisions based on what you *assume*, as that would not *only* be a disaster, but rather dangerous too.'

It was her turn to pull on her boots and grab her car keys. She ruffled Truffle's fur as she headed for the door. She had planned on going to the bistro later anyway, but suddenly wanted to put some distance between them.

'Where are you going?' he sounded off.

'Out!' Her churlish reply.

'Verty!'

He called after her, but it was too late; her mind was set on giving him some space, giving both of them some space. Jumping into the truck, she hit the accelerator and made her way along the track, past the lodge where Shaun and Arla were no doubt discussing their next move. She turned out onto the main road, and headed towards town, as both her speed and her pulse slowed. By the time she passed the 'Welcome To Linden Falls' sign she regretted storming out of the house, knowing how inadequate and irritating it felt when Sonny had done similar to her. She'd call Jack the moment she arrived; she would apologise and explain that she was at the bistro and would be home later.

Having parked in the town square, her intention was to head to The Crooked Porch, chat with Nicole, and seek out a slice of pie, knowing that, even after her hearty breakfast, the sugar hit would do her no harm. She was unsure there was anything she could easily snaffle in the fridge at Claudine's. How she hated rowing with her man, especially at a time like this. It left her with a cold kernel of sadness in her stomach from which branches sprouted and filled her up. This was not how they lived, in discord, without love!

She walked slowly, looking over at the chapel where only yesterday they had said goodbye to Debra. It was as if stress left her body as she walked beneath the beautiful big-blue Vermont sky with barely a wisp of cloud. The spring was doing its best to let summer in, and a warm breeze lifted her spirits as she strolled under the grand old linden tree from which the town took its name. As ever, handwritten wishes, tied to the branches, fluttered like unusual blooms as the wind encouraged them to dance. She wondered if Vera was free or fancied a chat, entirely grateful for the woman's friendship and guidance that was always offered without filter or agenda. A rare thing. That, and she wasn't looking forward to being in the bistro alone. It was a lot harder to return than she thought.

Verity ferreted in her jacket pocket for her phone when she spied a figure sitting on one of the benches that lined the square, head down, hands clasped. If she hadn't known any different, she might have thought he was in prayer. It felt at once both disloyal and opportune, a chance to talk to the man who had placed a tornado inside her marriage. The man sitting there was the man who had hurt Debra – the monster - and walked out on his young son.

'Todd?' she called as she approached, wanting to give him a chance to compose himself. It was startling just how much he looked like Shaun, unsurprising really, but still it threw her a little. What was surprising was how this monster looked like any other man in the street, a pale blue button-down Oxford, khakis, and slip on tan, suede Sebagos, neat hair, clean shaven. What did she expect? Horns?

He sat up abruptly and nervously wiped his palms on the thighs of his jeans.

'Hello.'

'Hi, I'm … I'm Verity, Jack's wife.' She cursed her nerves.

'Yes, I know.' His voice was soft, not bullish or aggressive as it had been in her imagination. 'I saw you yesterday, plus Shaun had posted about you and Jack getting hitched on Facebook. You're British, right?'

'Yes.' The fact he kept up with Shaun on Facebook was news.

'Funny you ended up here. A long way from home.' He looked around the town where the shop signs were quaint, the air clean, and the folks who went about their business did so with the raise of a neighbourly hand and smile.

'I guess it is, but it turns out this is home. I'm a firm believer that you end up where you are meant to be with the people you are meant to be with.'

'It's a nice thought.' He sighed, as if he didn't quite share her faith. 'What part of the UK are you from?'

'Erm, London, England, have you been?'

'Yes, yes.' He met her eyes briefly, then looked away. 'My … my wife and I travel a lot and we've been to London and Manchester where she has family.'

A wife! Another wife! Was he kind to her or did he hurt her too? Did Shaun have half-siblings? Again, she felt the bite of nerves as she waded further into unchartered waters.

'I raised a glass to you both when I read that you'd married.' He gave a brief smile. 'I'm happy Jack found you, settled down. He's a good man.'

She nodded, quite taken by his calm manner and warm tone, again not what she had expected at all. Aware as she was that even the calmest and warmest of exteriors could be the cloak behind which thoroughly rotten people hid. It was, however, easy to see how someone as sweet natured and trusting as Debra might be taken in by such a man.

'You follow Shaun on Facebook?' This was of interest to her.

'Yes, but under my wife's account. It sounds covert … I guess it is. I just like to see his pictures, know how he's doing. See my granddaughters.' He coughed to clear the break in his voice.

She could not imagine the horror of having to watch Sophie's life secretly from afar. She could also not imagine letting a man with such a temper near her grandchildren.

'Mind if I sit down?' She indicated the space on the bench

next to him and he scooted as far as he was able towards the end.

'Sure.'

She sat. He looked nervously over her shoulder, along the path,

'Jack's at home.'

The man exhaled, as if he'd been holding his breath.

'Hard to imagine we used to be such good friends, camping, and hiking when he was home; we'd sit on a rock with a view and talk about nothing. Then he introduced Deb and I.'

This she knew, understanding how the fact must in no small way contribute to Jack's feelings of guilt, wondering how often he must have relived the *what-if* moments of his sister's life.

'You're right; he is a good man,' she began, 'a man who's wrestling with a lot.'

'I thought it was important for me to come pay my respects, and, I can't lie, I hoped it might be a chance to clear the air, maybe. I don't know what I thought.' He ran his hand over his mouth.

'I think with all the high emotion that naturally surrounds a funeral, that might have been a bit of a stretch.' She noted the understatement.

'I guess so. I saw it as the first opportunity I've had, to talk to Jack and Shaun while they were together. I guess I didn't think it through.'

'You thought they might *want* to speak to you?' She was aware of her sarcastic tone, bothered by the man's assumption after all he had done.

'As I say, I ... I didn't really think it through. I suppose I was impatient.'

Verity actually laughed out loud. 'Not impatient enough to make contact with Shaun since he was seven, yet impatient enough to want to see him on the day he buried his mother?'

Todd twisted to face her, his expression earnest, and this for her was conflicting. She didn't want to feel even the smallest flicker of sympathy for him.

'It's complicated.'

'Oh, it's always complicated.' She held her nerve, hating this catchall that was as much of a cop out as it was insipid.

'Look, you seem like a nice lady, but you don't know anything at all about me. But what I can tell you … is that I loved her.' He took a beat, as if savouring the words. 'I loved Debs more than I knew was possible.'

'From what I've heard, you sure had a strange way of showing it!'

'I don't know what you have heard,' he blinked, 'but it's the truth. Deb and I used to say we were two caterpillars when we met, about as ungainly! She had blue eyes the colour of cornflowers,' Verity nodded, her sister-in-law's eyes had indeed been the most striking shade of blue, 'and how we loved each other, faults, and all. And we did. We really did. We used to say that, when the time was right, we'd evolve into butterflies and fly away. Well, I don't know about evolving into a butterfly, but when she held Shaun in her arms I'd never seen a face so beautiful. She had bloomed into something spectacular all right.' He took a deep breath. 'I would like to talk to Shaun, to Jack too. I'm not asking for anything more than a chance to talk to them. I will also respect their decision if they don't want to, and I will drive to the airport and be on the first plane out of here.'

'Is that why you're still here? To see them?' she asked quietly. His words, whether true or not, were moving.

The man nodded, 'Yes, and I wanted to go to visit the chapel today, to talk to Deb, say my goodbye, privately. And then I came here.'

'You found our famous wishing tree.'

'There must be a lot of wealthy, beautiful, happy, healthy souls around these parts!'

'I think you'd be surprised what people wish for.'

'How many wishes do you get?' She wasn't sure if he was being cynical or endearing.

'I guess whatever feels important enough to write down and hang on a branch. For some people that might be one thing, for others that might be many things.'

'I see.' He stared at the messages, fluttering as the breeze picked up.

She knew her own wish to start over and to be loved had certainly come true. In that moment she again regretted running out on Jack, feeling instantly disloyal to be chatting to this man, to be here at all. 'I don't know if Jack will see you, I just don't know.' She voiced her thoughts.

'And Shaun?' He almost pleaded.

'I don't know,' she shrugged. 'Look, whether I want to be or not, I am involved and so I'll try and sound them out. I'll call you at the inn if you like.'

'How do you know I'm staying at the inn?'

Verity stood and looked around her neighbourhood, 'This is Linden Falls; everyone knows everything .... I'll be in touch.'

'Thank you, Verity.'

'Don't thank me yet,' she responded over her shoulder, knowing the reception she was going to get from Jack was unlikely to be favourable when he heard her news.

With the key in her hand, she stood by the front door of Claudine's and took a deep breath. All she had to do was go inside, clean the kitchen, remove any out-of-date produce, check the larder and freezer and put an order in for the next dinner service. Yet no matter how much she ran through what needed to happen in her thoughts, she just couldn't do it. Her tears were as unexpected as they were cathartic, and she stood for a minute letting them fall.

'What a bloody mess!' she whispered as she lost her nerve and put the key back in her bag before walking briskly to the truck. A quick glance at the bench and there was no sign of Todd, for which she was entirely thankful.

Verity drove back slowly from town with her thoughts churning. She hated how complex and fragile the situation felt, doing her best to practice what she wanted to say and how she wanted to say it. The sun, high in the sky, filtered through the leaves to make dappled patterns revealing stars of daylight through the canopy above her. She followed the road which climbed sharply and took the second left at the sign for White Cedar Farm, a journey she had made hundreds of times, and yet it still thrilled her to turn up along the track and know that she was nearly home.

Jack was in the yard, axe in hand, splitting logs that he piled neatly and obsessively in their wood shed. She parked the truck and climbed out. Truffle, as ever, went crazy at the sight of her, tail wagging, panting with joy and pawing at her for affection, as if she had been gone for far too long.

'Hello, Truff, hello, baby girl!' She bent low and rubbed her dog's face and ears.

'See, Truff, I told you she'd come back.'

'I'll always come back.' She stood and smiled at her husband who buried the blade in the chopping block and walked over to her. He removed his baseball hat and stuffed it in his jeans pocket, before reaching out and pulling her towards him, holding her tightly and breathing into her hair.

'That's the thing, Verty, I'd rather you didn't go in the first place.'

'I'm sorry,' she whispered. 'I shouldn't have gone off like that.'

'No, I'm sorry. You're right, I shouldn't be taking it out on you. You are in fact the very last person in the world I should be taking anything out on. What would I do without you?'

'I pray you'll never have to find out.' She kissed his cheek. 'I do need to talk to you though. Come and sit with me.'

Taking his hand, she guided him to the porch where two

ancient, restored Adirondack chairs painted in the palest blue were positioned side by side, this the spot where they liked to have a sundowner and a catch up.

They sat.

'I'm just going to come right out with it.' She stared ahead, knowing it easier to broach such a topic that way than to face him. 'I saw him. I saw Todd.'

'Okay.' He offered nothing else, and it was therefore time for her to come completely clean.

'I … I spoke to him, in fact.'

'I see.' She saw him shift in the chair.

'Do you want to know what happened, what he said?' She turned to him now, his expression hard to read.

He nodded.

'I hadn't intended to see him, but he was sitting on one of the benches by the linden tree and it felt weird not to engage with him. I sat next to him on the bench. He told me he had wanted to say goodbye to Deb on his own today, and that things were complicated, he said he was married, and that he wanted to see you and Shaun, mainly Shaun, but you too.'

'Well, I don't want to see him.' He sat forward in the chair and rubbed his hands together. His tone resolute.

'For what it's worth, I think you should see him. I think you should both see him. It won't be easy, but so much better if you both got some sort of closure. A chance to get it all out in the open, say what needs to be said. Or maybe I only suggest that because it's what would work for me. I see the way it's eating you up and it feels like there is so much that's unresolved. I don't know, Jack, I guess I just want it not to fester like a wound that needs air.'

Jack shook his head and stared into the middle distance.

'I hear you, I do; the thing is, I'm doing my very best to keep on an even keel, trying real hard not to let my emotions get the better of me. So, I tell you what I'm going to do. I'm going to let Shaun decide. You speak to Shaun, tell him what you have told me, and if he wants to talk to the man, then I will be right by his side. But I tell you this, Verty,' he stood then and restored his baseball cap, no doubt ready to get back to chopping his logs, 'I pray to God he tells you that it's a bad, bad idea.'

CHAPTER 6

Verity was nervous. Beyond nervous. She could quite easily throw up at the thought of the evening ahead. This in no small part due to the fact that she was the architect of the reunion and all its dreadful possible outcomes that played out in her mind. She fully felt the weight of the responsibility.

When she had dropped in at the lodge earlier and explained that she'd seen Todd, Shaun had responded instantly and enthusiastically without hesitation.

'Yes, yes, I'll see him.'

'Are you sure, Shauny?' Arla voiced her concern, her expression quite tortured, and again Verity wondered if she had done the right thing.

'I'm sure. Who knows when I'll get the chance again, if ever?' He stared at his wife, who nodded.

'I just don't want you to get hurt,' Arla whispered.

'Baby,' Shaun smiled at his beloved, 'I've been hurting for years, and losing Mom means I am hurting more than I ever have. What harm can he do to me now?'

'Well, that's my worry.' Arla didn't shy away from this truth.

Jack had taken an altogether more reserved approach and had simply nodded when she told him of Shaun's decision and the fact that Todd was driving over that very evening.

'All right then,' his rather succinct response. He had then pretty much disappeared into the yard, whether working or avoiding her it was hard to tell; either way, his absence did nothing to help alleviate her nerves.

She had spent the intervening hours in a quandary. What to provide? A light supper? Drinks? Nibbles? Tea and biscuits? It wasn't as if there was a precedent for having a man her husband wanted to physically hurt inside their home as a guest, a man who had abandoned Shaun, hurt Debra, and who had turned up uninvited, out of the blue.

Jack showered and came down in clean jeans and a white shirt.

'You look nice.' She always thought so, knowing they were lucky that the flame of desire was well and truly lit even after seven years of marriage.

'Thanks.'

'How long is it since you last saw him?' she asked as they waited, standing in the kitchen with the lamps lit, Truffle snoring in her basket and one of Verity's more relaxed playlists floating through the speaker. Her efforts gave the illusion of serenity, but the atmosphere spoke of anything but. Jack had paced, opened and closed drawers, and sighed heavily.

'Um,' he looked skyward and did the calculation, 'twenty-odd years.'

'That's a long time.' The awkwardness and tension, most alien, reduced their conversation to the mundane.

'Yep.'

This was what he did during times of stress; he retreated verbally, as if he could keep everything at bay by not opening up, doing his best to control every aspect of his being, even his speech, especially his speech.

'Hello-o?' Shaun and Arla heralded their arrival.

'Hey, you two!' She stepped into the living area and smiled, relieved to have their company.

'I am so nervous,' Shaun exhaled loudly.

'I told him that Todd will be too and that he ain't got nothing to be nervous about.'

'Arla's right.' God, she hoped Arla was right!

'What do you reckon, Jack?' Shaun spoke directly to his uncle. 'You and me stand either side of the front door and clothes line him as he walks in?'

'Don't tempt me.'

Shaun's attempt at humour fell flat, as Jack folded his arms across his chest. It was then they heard the sound of a car pulling up on the track and his arms fell to his sides, his fingers flexed. Shaun gasped, as if struck. Arla walked forward and took her husband's hand and Verity felt the crushing doubt that it was a good idea to have the man in their home, again silently cursing her part in it and wishing she were not putting her husband through this. It was, however, a little late for that.

The four stood, a guard of honour, all awkwardly transfixed by the entrance. It was mere minutes later that she saw the outline of their guest, who now knocked.

'I'll go.' Jack pulled his shoulders back, and she stared as he opened the door and the two men, once the best of friends, stared at each other.

'Jack.' Todd held out his hand and there was a second where her heart was in her mouth, wondering how her husband might respond. Her husband bristled, but shook Todd's hand briefly, and stood back to allow the man entry.

'Wow,' Todd whispered, then stared at Shaun and did nothing to try and disguise the tears that almost instantly sheeted his face. 'I swore I wasn't going to do this.' He wiped his face. 'Look at you!' He took a step forward and Shaun, almost instinctively, took one back. She thought for one terrible moment that Todd might fall over as he seemed to lose his footfall and stumbled on the spot. 'I … I didn't know what to bring, so,' he handed Verity a bottle of sparkling apple juice and some handmade chocolates.

'Thank you.' She was gracious, but kept her voice clipped, denying her natural warmth that such an arrival and gift would ordinarily warrant, wanting Jack to know at every moment that she was on his side, always on his side. 'Can I get you something to drink?'

'No, no, thank you.' Todd placed his hand on his stomach as if he too might be fighting the urge to vomit his nerves.

'Why don't we all sit down?' she suggested, hoping that when seated there might be a dent in the formality that gave the room a weighted atmosphere.

She had assumed that they would sit in the den or lounge, but, instead, Jack walked to the dining table and sat down. Shaun sat next to him, and Arla sat on the other side of the table to Shaun, facing him. Verity followed their lead and sat opposite Jack, indicating to Todd who took the seat at the head of the table, as far as it was possible to sit from Jack but also looking horribly exposed, as if he were there for an interrogation, which, of course, in one sense he was.

'Thank you for, for asking me over. I … I don't know what to say, where to start.' Todd licked his dry lips, never taking his eyes off Shaun.

'That makes two of us.' Shaun stated, unflinching, jaw tense.

'I thought, erm, I thought the funeral yesterday was …' it seemed Todd ran out of adjectives, 'you did her proud.'

Jack snorted his derision and Verity coughed, as if she might be able to disguise the noise, hide it.

'It's been a long time, Jack.' Todd persevered.

'Yep.'

'I can't stop staring at you, Shaun. I'm sorry.' Todd, once

again visibly moved, wiped his face. 'I have dreamed of this moment.'

'I guess my thought is,' Shaun began, paying no heed to his father's dream, 'that it wouldn't have been that hard for you to track me down, had you really wanted to. But I guess it wasn't that straightforward, you must have known the reception you'd get.'

'I didn't have to track you down, son.' He used the word without flinching and she saw Shaun's eyes widen. 'I knew where you were. I *always* knew how you were.'

'You did?' Shaun swallowed.

'Yes, always,' he reiterated.

'Well, you have the advantage then, as I didn't know if you were living a few doors down, in prison, working abroad or dead in a ditch! And that's how it's always been. You've been no more than a shadowy memory since I was a kid.'

'You sound so angry,' Todd spoke softly, not in judgement, it seemed, but more in sad realisation.

'You expected different?' Shaun spat, as Arla knitted her hands on the tabletop.

'No, no, sir, I did not. But that doesn't mean it cuts me any less.' Todd spoke with a frankness that she couldn't help but admire.

'You think you can show up here and waltz in like everything is good?' Shaun spoke with the embers of hurt glowing in his voice.

'No,' again Todd shook his head. 'I don't, but I do want the chance to—'

'Good,' Shaun cut him off, 'cos you say you know where I've been, but you know nothing about me! You know nothing about me since I was seven years old!'

'I know more than you think.' Todd smiled weakly.

'Oh, yeah? Was that from all the parent teacher meetings you rushed home for? The sports meets. Or maybe from reading my Christmas lists to Santa? Or was it the speech I gave at my wedding?'

'Trust me. I wish, more than I can ever express, that I had had the chance to be there for all of those things—'

'Trust you?' Shaun gave a wry laugh, ignoring the man's wish so openly expressed.

Todd was silent for a beat, letting the air settle.

'I knew all about your schooling, Shaun. I kept direct contact with the staff, and I had copies of all your report cards. With Debra's blessing, of course. She also sent me any mention in a newspaper, like the time you smashed the eight hundred meters record for the county! Boy that was some day!' Todd shook his head, his eyes bright with pride.

'Mom … Mom sent you stuff?' Shaun sat up in the chair, as did Jack. This was clearly news.

'Yes, lots of it. I have a whole bureau full. I'm married.' He paused, looking around the table, as if to see how the fact landed. 'My wife, Lindsey, she thought it best I came alone, but she sends her condolences. She reads everything Deb sends. Sent,' he corrected with an almost wistful tone. 'Lindsey feels like she knows you, as do I. Even though, seeing you now, it's obvious we have a lot of work to do, a lot to cover.'

Jack sat up straight, the chair creaked, and Todd went quiet, as if aware that to talk of the future, to make any assumption might be overstepping the mark.

Shaun stared at the man, his chest heaving, 'Do you … do you and Lindsey have kids?'

'Only you.'

'Why, why would Mom do that? Why would she send you stuff for all those years?' Shaun asked aloud but his tone suggested it might be a question for himself.

'Because I'm your daddy.' Todd's voice quavered. 'No matter how far away, I always was and always will be your daddy.'

It was a touching moment, not that her husband seemed remotely stirred by it.

'It takes more than a name on a birth certificate to be a father, Todd,' Jack interjected. 'It's about showing up!'

Verity knew he spoke from experience and had been showing up for his nephew his whole life, as he now did for Sophie. She just wished his anger would calm for a minute, knowing this kind of open conversation was how things moved forward, how they reached closure, no matter how painful.

'Deb never wanted me to show up; she asked me not to.' He nodded.

'And can you blame her?' Jack continued, 'Being a father is about more than just being there, it's about the basics, like … erm, let me think …' he tapped his chin, 'how about not beating on the child's mother!'

There. He had done it. Pulled off the Band-Aid and exposed the wound. And it hurt. It hurt them all to hear it and to witness it.

'Beat on his mother?' Todd stared at Jack, his mouth open, before he sat up straight and took a deep breath. 'You know, Jack, you and I used to be friends.' Todd looked straight at him. 'All those hours out in the wilds, finding a place to perch and talking til the sun came up.'

'Used to be is correct. And I guess that's why I have nothing but contempt for you and why I am so mad at myself. You fooled us all!'

'You honestly think I'm capable of *hurting* Debs?' he asked, twisting his hands together. 'You think I could *do* something like that? You know me, Jack! You know me! You stood at *my* wedding and said in front of your mom and dad and *my* mom and dad how you would pick me to look after your little sister, that's what you said!'

'We all said a lot of things back then. I seem to remember you standing in a church and saying that you'd love and cherish her till death did you part. Do you remember that?'

'Of course I remember that!'

'Or how about forsaking all others? You remember *that* part?' Jack spoke with derision and Todd shrank accordingly.

'I regret so much,' Todd spoke softly, his shoulders hunched, as if the whole experience was agonizing, 'but hurt her?' He shook his head.

'I heard it.' Shaun spoke softly, yet firmly, as if unable to stand it any longer. 'I heard what happened that night, and then you left, and she shut the door and that was that!'

'It's not what you think,' Todd's arms flailed as if he wanted to reach for his son but was aware that there was a cavernous valley between them. 'It's not, Shaun, I—'

'I need to, I need to go now!' Shaun jumped up, as if suddenly quite overwhelmed, and her heart ached for him. He walked to the door, pausing only to let Arla catch up.

'Bye,' Arla gave a small wave over her shoulder as they left.

They closed the door hard enough to make Truffle bark.

'Settle down, darling!' she called, knowing a barking Truffle would do nothing to ease the tension.

Shaun leaving changed the dynamic; Todd slumped a little as if deflated. Verity knew that if Jack weren't being so defensive, this was the moment she would offer solace and try to smooth things. Todd, it seemed, felt similarly.

'I am sorry for your loss, Jack, I know how close you and Deb were.'

Jack drummed his fingers on the tabletop as if he couldn't care less about what Todd had to say or his opinions.

'I couldn't believe it when Andrea called me.'

'Andrea called you?' Jack sounded surprised.

'Who's Andrea?' It was a name she hadn't heard before.

'Andrea and Deb were at school together. She lives in Melbourne now, sent flowers.' Jack filled her in.

'Oh, right.' She smiled, so many beautiful flowers.

'Shaun had let her know apparently and so she called me. We've kept in touch.' Jack stiffened at this news; she knew he would see this as disloyal on Andrea's part. 'I told her how I'd spoken to Deb only a few months back.'

'Now why would she speak to you?' Jack asked directly.

'She told me she wanted to write to me and asked if we were at the same address in Raleigh, as she didn't want the letter to go astray.'

'What did she want to write to you about?'

Even she felt this question to be a little invasive.

Todd double blinked at the man who had been his brother-in-law and continued in his unhurried pace, 'A … a private matter.'

'Well, you could say anything! My sister ain't exactly here to defend herself! All this baloney about school reports and keeping in touch!'

'Why would I?' Todd asked. 'Why would I come all this way, after all this time, to run her into the ground or make stuff up? Why would I?'

'I don't know, Todd. I guess they're the very questions I'm asking myself.' Jack stared at him.

'I loved her.' Todd swallowed, trying to steady his voice. 'I *loved* her, and in those early days, I had pretty much everything I had ever wanted and more,' he paused to quell the tremble to his bottom lip. 'When she got pregnant, you saw how we were, Jack, you *know*!'

Verity watched her husband look downwards, and she understood that to recall that time might just be too painful.

'It was the most wonderful thing; we were so excited. Shaun was a good baby, he slept, he fed, he was content, but' Todd shook his head, 'Deb wasn't. She wasn't happy or content, she was the opposite, fretful, sad, and I couldn't understand it. And I couldn't make it right; Lord knows I tried. That baby boy,' he glanced at Verity, 'that baby boy was the thing she had always longed for, me too, to be a daddy! It was the greatest thing I could have imagined. And pride! Wow, they say pride is a sin, but I could no more dampen that feeling than I could fly to the moon. Every time I got to say, "That's my son, my boy, Shaun Darby Miller."' He stopped to reach for the handkerchief in his pocket and wiped his eyes. 'And to see him sitting there today, a fine man, with that look of fire in his eyes when he looked at me,' he took a minute, 'I know it will take me a while to get over.'

'This is all very interesting,' Jack spoke slowly, as if disinterested, and Verity fixed him with a knowing stare; he had agreed to keep it civil, agreed to let Todd say his piece.

'Deb was unwell, Jack. Postnatal depression, I now believe, but I'll be darned if I'd even heard of such a thing. She had violent mood swings, was medicated which only made things worse. And I … I did wrong.' He placed his palms on the table as if taking an oath. 'I know I did wrong. I had a relationship with a co-worker, not even a relationship. A couple of hookups. Man, was I lonely.'

It was always an easy defence - the loneliness, the fact that your spouse was neglecting you, neglecting themselves or any number of variants that all added up to the same thing, infidelity. Having been on the receiving end when Sonny had an affair, she knew the reasoning was almost secondary, it hurt just the same. She could only imagine the effect it must have had on Debra who by the sounds of it was already suffering greatly.

'I would regularly wake in the night to find Deb in a fit of rage. She'd hit me, slap me. I'd be dreaming and the next minute find myself being attacked. I was scared of her and scared for her. Scared for Shaun too. We rowed one night, and I told her, told her I was seeing someone from work, no more than a fling, but no less damaging for that and she went,' he took a moment, 'she went crazy. Absolutely nuts! She attacked me, punching, and kicking, lashing out! She broke the glass of the cabinet, smashed up the room. I was begging her to stop, I would never – could never – lay a finger on her, but I didn't know how to make it stop. She said I was the reason she was so angry, called me all the names she could lay her tongue to, and told me to get the hell out. I was bleeding; I saw my blood on the rug in the hall my parents had bought us for a wedding gift, and I knew, I knew that if we were to stand any chance, I needed to get away from the violence and she needed to be away from me, and I needed her to get help - and she did.' He looked up, and she got the impression he didn't often speak this freely. 'She did.'

Verity was watching Jack, who stared, his expression hard to read. His breathing seemed a little laboured.

'I was ashamed of being beaten, ashamed of cheating on her, ashamed for walking out. She told me if I ever returned she'd run, and she'd take Shaun and I'd never find them, and I believed her. After a while, we kept in touch, she'd write, always telling me how our son was doing and telling me how she was getting better. I always sent money, right up until Shaun left home, I sent money. She didn't want me back and I respected that. She asked me not to contact Shaun, said it would be unsettling for them both, and I respected that too. I then met my wife, Lindsey, and she helped me make sense of it all. But in recent years, I find it hard to respect the choices that were made on my behalf because I miss my son. I miss him! And I've missed you, Jack. I have grandbabies I've never met who know nothing about me. My crime was cheating on Debra, and I have always put my hands up to that, but nothing more. And for that I think I've paid a heavy price.'

Verity was stunned into silence, going over the new facts that Todd had shared and wondering what to make of it all. His last words lingered; he had indeed paid a heavy price ....

'As I said, Todd, my sister is not here to defend herself.' Jack spoke calmly.

She didn't know what to say! Wary of sounding disloyal

but equally appalled that her husband gave the man's words so little credence.

'I'm about done here.' Her husband stood. 'Verity, can you show our *guest* out?'

Todd stood, his face flushed red, as he too seemingly felt the cloak of embarrassment about his shoulders.

Todd put his hands in the air, 'I think maybe this was a mistake. Thank you, for your ... for your hospitality.' Nervously, he addressed Verity. 'I would like to leave Shaun my address and contact details. Do you think that would be okay?'

'Leave them at the inn. They'll pass them on if Shaun wants them.' This Jack's final attack.

Verity saw the man off and watched his hire car career off down the track.

'It's bullshit!' Jack announced the moment she walked back inside. 'Debra was a great mom, she loved Shaun, she—'

Verity put her hands up to stop him,

'Don't say another word. Please, Jack, not tonight.'

CHAPTER 7

Verity woke to find Jack's side of the bed was empty. She threw on her housecoat and went in search of coffee. Jack had, as ever, prepped the machine. There were bookings for the bistro tomorrow night and it was about time she started to think about the menu. There was a note by her favourite mug:

TAKEN TRUFFLE OUT TO CHECK THE FENCES x

She was thankful for the addition of a kiss. They had lay in silence last night, most unlike them; even Truffle stayed downstairs in her cozy basket rather than come and imbibe the frosty atmosphere that hovered like mist on the morn in their bedroom. They had rowed before, of course they had, bickered, fought, but it was always a short, nonsensical blast, usually with its roots in tiredness, a fatigue that bred rattiness.

This felt different. Grief was an unpredictable master and, with the whole Todd fiasco thrown into the mix, she felt for the first time in their marriage that she was on a shaky platform. Not that they were going to implode, nothing like that. It would pass, she was confident; they were too strong, and had waited too long to find each other for there to be any other outcome, but that didn't make it any less uncomfortable right now.

'Morning, Verity. The door was open, so,' Shaun's wife pointed down the hallway.

'Arla, hello, darling, yes, of course, come in, come in! Please excuse me still in my pj's!'

Arla flapped her hand, 'Don't worry about it, I sometimes do the school run with mine tucked into my jeans.'

'When Sophie was little, she was at school in Chelsea and some of the mums would be done up to the nines, hair, makeup, clothes, all on point and I would pitch up having pulled a fifteen-hour shift at the restaurant, fallen into bed at two a.m. smelling of garlic and wearing yesterday's makeup. Those women would look at me with such pity it was galling. I had very few mum-at-the-gate friends, only a couple, in fact, but they were women like me without time or inclination to worry about aesthetics.'

'It doesn't sound like my kinda crowd.' Arla pulled a face.

'Oh, darling, they weren't my kinda crowd either! That's why I love it here.'

They both laughed.

'How's Shaun doing?' She pressed the button for coffee and reloaded it for her guest.

'How's he, how am *I*? That was quite some night.' Arla rolled her eyes.

'You can say that again.'

'He's … quiet. Thinking it all through, I guess.' Arla fidgeted with her wedding ring. 'What did Todd say after we'd left?'

'A lot.' She wondered just how much of it was her place to share. 'He suggested there was more to he and Deb divorcing than Jack and Shaun might have been aware. I don't know. I think Jack should talk to Shaun.' She was overly wary of saying or doing the wrong thing.

'We had no idea that Deb had shared so much of Shaun's childhood with his dad; it felt kinda nice and kinda sad at the same time. I mean he was either a bad, bad man or he wasn't, you know? Or maybe Deb forgave him, and if she could forgive him …'

Verity handed Arla her coffee.

'Thanks.'

'I understand, and, at the risk of sounding cliché, I think it was complicated.'

Arla followed her to the couch in the snug where they sat facing each other.

'I haven't said this to Shaun, but I felt a bit sorry for Todd.'

'And I daren't say as much to Jack, but me too.'

It felt nice to share the connection, if not a little conspiratorial.

Arla nodded. 'But then I feel so guilty because Deb was just wonderful. I loved her so much.'

'We all did, honey, but that doesn't mean we can't have sympathy for the most awful of situations. If Todd was violent towards her then my blood boils; no woman, no *person*, should go through that, to be made to feel less than. And the fact it all ended so bitterly, so abruptly, just awful for everyone.' She sipped her coffee.

'You said *if* Todd was violent; you think that might not be true?' Arla stared at her, and she felt the intensity in it.

'Arla,' she exhaled, 'I just don't know.' She spoke the truth. 'If he was, then my heart breaks for Deb and Shaun; if he didn't, my heart breaks for all of them.' Verity's heart, broken or not, was with any woman who had felt the effects of postnatal depression and all that came with that, the guilt, the shame, the lack of understanding. How she wished she had been around back then to help.

'What a mess.' The young woman took a glug of coffee

and Verity acknowledged the understatement. 'We're heading back this morning. Shaun wants to get back to the girls.'

'You know we're here for you guys, always.' Verity reached out and put her hand on Arla's arm.

'We do. Shaun's head is spinning, I think it best he lets everything settle and then starts asking the questions he needs to.'

'I think that's smart.' She smiled at the woman who had a good head on her shoulders. 'It's been so lovely to see you both, even under these horrible circumstances.'

Arla finished her coffee and stood. 'We'll pack up and come say bye.'

'Yes, Jack shouldn't be too much longer.'

'He seems …' Arla hesitated, and Verity could only stare at her, knowing that, yes, he did ….

With her guests gone and Jack out repairing stock fencing on their boundary, Verity made her way into town to get up on some bits and pieces at the store. There were buffet leftovers to use up and she figured with just a few key ingredients she could recycle them into something edible. They were out of eggs, milk and orange juice, and she was out of enthusiasm for the task as her truck tootled into town. It was as she thought about where to park that her phone buzzed in its holder on her dash.

'Vera!'

'Hey, Verity, watcha doin?'

'Just coming into town actually; need to go to the store.'

'Oh, perfect. Fancy a coffee?'

'Have you met me? I always fancy a coffee!' she smiled.

'That's what I thought. Come to the salon; I've got no one in until three and Mira is away for couple of days.'

Mira, who had worked for Vera for a number of years now, was now a partner in the hair and beauty salon. An arrangement that suited them both, as they shared the workload and the profits, allowing each the time to enjoy a life beyond the salon walls. For Vera, this meant weekends away to see her son, Knox, his wife, Ashley, and their adorable little boy, Carter, who all lived in Ithaca. It also meant she could accompany Wyatt on his work trips out of state.

Verity found a spot and parked up not far from Vera's premises. She felt her bones relax as she pushed open the door of the salon and walked into the small space that smelled of shampoo, scented candles and the chemicals that ensured straight hair was curled, curly hair was straightened, thin hair was thickened up and wild hair was tamed.

Vera, amazed still, often commented that, *'No one is content with the head of hair that the good Lord has given them! Which is a real good thing, or I'd be out of business!'*

It used to make Verity laugh. She always kept to herself the fact that hair, she felt, had a lot more to do with genetics than the Lord.

'Here she is!' Vera walked forward and handed her a big mug.

'Now, that's what I call service. Our usual chairs?'

'Why not?' Vera led the way and the two women settled into the deep leather seats in front of the mirrors where ordinarily they would find themselves pampered.

'Do you know, I think this is the only time I look at myself, I mean properly study myself, when I'm having my hair done. Otherwise, it's a quick squizz in the mirror, where the first thing I see is the map of the Nile delta on my forehead and so I look away, shove my hair into a messy knot and go about my day.' Verity spoke as she ran her fingertips over the tributary of lines that gathered in the corners of her eyes and ran proudly from her top lip.

'I look in the mirror all the time!' Vera laughed, 'not because I'm vain, although I might be a bit, but because it's how I talk to my customers, both staring at our reflections. I do it so often that it's a surprise for me to find this mole on the side of my face is actually on the right and not the left!'

'Did you hear about Deb's ex-husband staying at the inn?' She wanted her friend's take on things.

'I might have heard something ...' Vera sipped her coffee, not one for idle gossip.

'It's thrown Jack for a loop, I can tell you.'

'It's *what* now?' Vera stared at her before they both laughed.

'Confused him, shocked him, thrown him off course,' she translated.

'I bet it has.'

She proceeded with caution. Even though Vera was her great friend, she knew that Deb's story – indeed Todd's story – was not hers to tell.

'Deb didn't talk to me much about her life with Todd, didn't really dwell on life before Linden Falls. But it doesn't sound like she had the best time.'

'She sure didn't.' Vera lowered her voice, 'I knew she and Todd split up when their boy was young. I asked her once why she didn't ever get back in the saddle, told her if she decided to get out there, there'd be a queue right round the block! I mean, come on, Verity, if an old woman like me can find love again ....'

'There's nothing old about you, Vera.' She smiled at the reflection of her very attractive friend.

'Except my creaking knees and my birth certificate that's been knocking around for a good few years now!' They both chuckled. 'It was strange, though, when I said that to Deb about maybe wanting to meet a companion, her reply has stayed with me.'

'Why? What did she say?' she leaned forward in the seat, interested.

'She said to put someone through that again would be the very worst thing she could imagine. I told her that not all men were like that and that she might get lucky and strike gold, I mean look at Wyatt and Jack, both good, good men! And then she said,' Vera hesitated. 'Then she said, "I'm not talking about all men or even one man, I'm talking about me."'

'What did she mean?' She spoke the thought aloud, stringing it to Todd's version of events that had brought more questions to their door than it had answered.

'I don't know, but it struck me at the time as a bit odd.' Vera sighed.

'Yes, it is.'

'Though Lord knows I will miss her smiling face,' the woman changed tack. 'I can't believe she's never going to walk through that door again.' Reaching forward, Vera plucked a tissue from the box and dabbed under her mascaraed lashes.

'She loved you.' Verity spoke the truth and hoped it helped.

'And I her. Why is death so shitty?' Vera sniffed.

'Because we are never prepared for it, and we can't imagine it happening to us.'

'I think the opposite,' Vera stared at her in the mirror. 'I think it makes us sad because we can imagine it happening to us.'

'You might be right.' Verity sipped her coffee and wanted suddenly to get home to Jack, knowing that each day, each minute, was precious.

As dusk fell at White Cedar Farm, Verity was overcome with tiredness. It had been a long day on top of a long week, and she was still trying to psych herself up for opening up the bistro tomorrow. Having waved Shaun and Arla off to head to the airport, Jack had done his level best to keep busy, and crucially keep out of her way. Or maybe she was being unfair; he did always have a thousand chores to do, but, on any ordinary day, those chores would be interspersed with lunch, chats, cups of tea, a kiss on the cheek before he went back outside, and he would whistle and sing as he went. Today everything was a little stilted, a little cool, and she hated it. When things weren't right between them, it felt as if the world was a little thrown off its axis.

With the dishwasher whirring, Truffle snoring, and the supper leftovers of mac and cheese popped into the fridge ready to be eaten for lunch tomorrow, she sat on the porch and was thankful that Jack joined her.

'How are you feeling?' she asked softly.

'Thoughtful.'

'Do you want to talk about it?' She curled her legs beneath her.

'Not really.' He met her gaze. 'And I don't mean that in a harsh way, I just—'

The telephone in the kitchen rang. She jumped up and went inside.

'Hello?'

'Verity, it's Janie,' Neva's niece who now ran the inn.

'Hi, Janie, is everything okay?' She was unaware of the woman ever calling her before; instantly she felt the flare of concern that something might have happened to Neva or Henry.

'I'm not sure,' this response did little to settle her nerves. Janie continued, 'You know we've had Deb's ex staying here.'

'I do, yes.'

'Well, I just had a call from his wife, asking if we'd heard from him. He seems to have gone missing.'

'What?' Verity closed her eyes. The bloody drama continued.

'She's left a number and I'd said I'd pass it on. She asked if you or Jack might make contact. I wasn't really sure what to say ....'

'No, I bet. Maybe I should call her …' Verity spoke aloud. 'Give me her number, lovey.' She grabbed the pen from the mug in which she kept a bouquet of pens and pencils and a note block, and wrote as Janie read aloud:

'919 870….'

'Who was it?' Jack asked as she put the phone down. He leaned against the counter.

'It was Janie from the inn; Todd's wife called her, trying to track him down.'

'Well, whaddya know? The cheater goes missing. Again!' He tutted.

She did her best to quell her irritation. 'It felt like more than that. I've got her number.'

'And you're going to call her, aren't you?' He shook his head and clicked his tongue against the roof of his mouth. It was simultaneously disapproving and judgemental, and she really didn't like it.

'Do you know, Jack, I'm not enjoying this feeling like I'm between a rock and a hard place. I am sick of it. You and I are on the same team, and I shouldn't have to censor what I think or what I want to say; that's not how we operate!' She hated the jump in her pulse. 'Todd's wife has never done any wrong to you or I or Deb – as far as we know. I don't see what the harm is in calling her!'

'So, call her. You're going to anyway with or without my input.' He whistled for Truffle who jumped out of her basket on command, always ready for a stroll with Jack.

Verity waited until he had left and let her pulse settle. She punched the number into her cell and took a deep breath.

'Hi, is that Lindsey?' she asked tentatively.

'Yes, is this Jack's wife?'

'Oh, yes!' Verity was a little taken aback, thinking she might have to introduce herself.

'Don't sound so surprised. I knew you were British, and I did ask the woman at Todd's hotel if you might call.'

'Well, when you put it like that,' she gave a small laugh, as befitting of her nerves. 'Is everything okay?'

'No,' the woman's voice faltered, 'everything is not okay. Todd told me he was leaving Linden Falls and checked out of where he was staying. I went to the airport, his flight landed, but he wasn't on it. I haven't heard from him since and I'm at my wits' end; this is so unlike him!'

'Gosh, well, I'm sure there'll be a reasonable explanation; maybe he simply missed the flight or—'

'Possibly, but I'm sure he'd call or text me. We talk all the time; we don't like to be apart from each other.'

It didn't sound like the words of a woman who was unhappy in her marriage, the exact opposite in fact.

'I just thought you might be able to shed some light; I wondered, hoped actually, that he might have dropped in to see Shaun on his way to the airport and time had run away with him ....' The woman's voice trailed off.

'No, no, as far as I'm aware we haven't seen him since about this time yesterday evening; he came over to our house. Shaun and his wife left earlier today.

'Yes, Todd said.' Lindsey's clipped tone suggested he had told her exactly how it went.

'I'm not sure what to suggest. Let me talk to Jack when he gets back, and I promise I'll let you know if I hear anything at all.'

'Thank you. It's Verity, right?'

'Yes, and try not to worry. You know the phrase, don't worry until you know you have something to worry about, easy to say, I know ....' Nerves encouraged her to gabble.

It was then she heard the sound of crying down the line.

'I'm doing nothing but worry. You know when your instinct tells you that you *do* have something to worry about?'

'I do, yes.'

'Well, it's just like that.'

Despite having never met Lindsey, Verity felt the pull of sympathy for her, the woman's anxiety and concern wrapped every word. Verity spoke softly, as she would if it were a friend she was trying to placate.

'You know, Lindsey, he will likely turn up and have no idea that you've been fretting. There is usually a simple explanation.'

'I keep telling myself that too, and yet ....' The woman's laugh was short and ironic.

'I promise to call you if I hear anything, and if he turns up, do drop me a text.'

'Sure thing, and thank you, Verity, for being so kind to us both.'

It seemed apparent Todd had told her that the warm welcome wasn't from everyone when he visited.

Lindsey spoke again, slowly, as if making the decision to trust her.

'He's been through hell and back.'

Debra too .... This thought she kept to herself.

'He had no idea that he had been branded as a monster. He thought his cheating was what spurred indifference from Shaun, the reason Debra never really forgave him, but to hear that everyone, Jack included, believed he had ... had *hurt* her,' Lindsey stuttered her distress. 'He tried to do his best by her and Shaun, he sent money we didn't have, every single month, and he wrote to Shaun, but he got nothing, not even a birthday card.'

The woman painted a pitiful picture.

'I wanted kids, but Todd always said he couldn't stand the idea of Shaun hearing about him with a new family, seeing pictures of Todd at the beach or out camping with his siblings who would be strangers, as if he'd been replaced. He said he could never do that to the boy, and I understood. But I also know he's never stopped hoping, praying that there might come a time for reconciliation. Everyone lost out.

Debra's passing is a sad, sad thing and my heart goes out to you all, but I'd be lying if I didn't admit that we saw this as an opportunity, a chance for Todd to maybe step in and find a way back to Shaun, back to Jack too.'

'I want to ask you something, something that might be insensitive or,' Verity wasn't sure how to proceed.

'Do I think Todd hit Debra? Did he beat on her? Is that what you want to ask me?' Lindsey sounded aggrieved.

'Yes, do you think it's possible?'

'No. It's not. It's not possible.' She spoke emphatically. 'He is not capable! I'd stake my life on it! He made some dumb mistakes, but, no! In fact, I know it's not true. Debra wrote to him a few months ago. I have the letter right here. She apologised. Her words were honest, heartfelt, and her sadness over it all is so clear. Not that Todd held on to any malice; he's not like that. He's kind. Really kind.'

Verity let out a long sigh.

'I think until Jack sees proof, has the story laid out in black and white then he will refuse to believe what happened. My heart breaks for them both. Deb going through something terrible, her mind unreliable when she was a new mum, which is a lot to cope with anyway, and Todd, thinking he had life figured out and then a sledgehammer coming in and cracking it wide open.'

'It's true, I feel sorry for them both too. But mostly I think about what Shaun lost because, no matter what happens, they can never get those years back.'

'No, no, they can't.' It was as sad as it was complicated. 'Lindsey, I'll call you if I hear anything. You have my cell number now. Please call too.'

Verity took a mug of tea to the porch and settled into the Adirondack chair with a small, embroidered cushion behind her back. It was as she waited for Jack and Truffle that her phone beeped, a text from Lindsey, and not just a text but pictures too.

Verity opened them and knew instantly what she was looking at, photographs of letters, the letters Debra had sent to Todd. It felt at once invasive and compelling to read the words her sister-in-law had written. She scanned them, feeling the same guilt as if she were looking at someone's diary or reading a love letter meant for someone else.

... I can only say that I was out of my mind. The scariest time of my life ...
It hurt so bad that you had disregarded our marriage vows so easily.
I was already in a ship without a rudder, lost at sea, and this news saw me smash upon the rocks ... entirely broken.
... that night when I attacked you, I wanted you gone, I wanted to be alone ...
... I can't believe I hurt you. Can't say sorry enough for all the hurt ...
... I am so sorry, Todd; I am not that person! I was never that person ...
... I can hardly stand to think of it ...
... the damage I have done ...

'Hey.'

She hadn't heard Jack come up the lane, and hastily put her phone face down on the arm of the chair.

'Hi,' she smiled and rubbed Truffle's head before the pup lay on down between the chairs and almost instantly fell asleep. How Verity envied her that skill.

'So did you call her?' Jack scratched his stubble.

'I did.'

He sat down hard in the chair next to her.

'I want to show you something, Jack. I want you to read something that she has just sent me.'

'What is it?' He sounded impatient, a forerunner to indifference that she recognised.

'It's letters from Deb, one of which is the letter Deb wrote to Todd a couple of months ago. The one he mentioned last night.'

'I don't want to read it.'

'Well, I think you maybe should.' She handed him her phone. 'I'll leave you to it.'

Verity made her way up the stairs and let the shower wash away the grime of another energy-sapping day. She hoped that Shaun and Arla were home safely with their little girls, and she hoped that Lindsey was, by now, reunited with her husband, but mainly she hoped that Jack would find some kind of peace in knowing the truth. She hoped a lot of things.

Her pyjamas were good for a second night, and she liked the softness of them against her clean skin. With her hair brushed, night cream applied to her face, neck, and hands and her housecoat on, she trod the stairs and went to find Jack and Truffle. No longer on the porch, she spied them out by the firepit on the brow of the hill; flames flickered and distorted the horizon. Jack took comfort from fire in the way she did from staring at the sea. Grabbing two wool blankets from the basket in which they lived, her bare feet made no sound as she approached, enabling her to hear the unmistakable, yet rare, sound of her husband crying. This, much more than the misty-eyed surges of emotion that had dogged him since the loss of his sister, was instead huge gulps of distress that were as hard to hear as they were, no doubt, cathartic.

Truffle lifted her head to welcome her, alerting Jack in the process. Leaning forward on the wide log on which he sat, he placed his head in his hands. Verity sank down to the dirt floor in front of him and held him tightly, as he cried. She wasn't sure how long they sat like that, five minutes, ten … but enough time for her husband to run out of tears and to allow his breathing to return to a normal rhythm. Eventually, as her leg began to cramp, she released the man she loved and took her place by his side. They sat in a comfortable silence, for which she was thankful, both allowing the facts to percolate, and he, like her, no doubt wondering where they went from here.

'She lied to me,' he began. 'Deb lied to me for such a long time.'

'She would have had her reasons.' This truth she offered to placate. 'I guess it must have been as hard to admit to it, but just as hard to live with.'

Jack took his time, rubbing his palms together as the fire sent flame fairies spiralling up into the night sky and the logs crackled, as she reached for the thick, soft blankets and placed one around his shoulders and one around her own. It was instantly comforting.

'If I had happened across Todd in any of the intervening years, God only knows what I might have done. I've carried this hatred towards him, and it wiped out our friendship, our history, everything.'

'You read the letter, Jack. Deb was sorry, so sorry.' She now felt obligated to fight from the corner of the woman they all loved and would miss and was not here to defend herself.

'It's not only that she lied to me, but she also lied to Shaun too.'

'Shaun adored her. And she him.'

'But that's the point, Verty. He wasn't given the opportunity to adore his father. She took that from him, took it from them both.'

'I don't want to keep defending her actions—'

'Yet it sounds like you might be about to, and, trust me, I want you to, because thinking negatively about my sister who has died is the worst feeling in the world!' He held her eye line in an expression that was without the sharp-eyed hostility that had gilded his words over the last few days; this was a new, more conciliatory phase and she was grateful for that.

'I only wanted to say that we don't know what she was thinking or why she acted as she did, but postnatal depression, any depression, can be a very dark thing and I should imagine a very lonely place. And the choices Deb made she had to live with until the day she died. Lindsey said earlier how everyone lost out, and I think that about sums it up.'

'We'll never know the reasons, will we? Never get to hear Deb give her version of events.' He looked into the middle distance as if this might be a moment of realisation.

'Nope. But one thing I do know is that she was your sister. She loved you very much, and you loved her. She might not have been perfect, but who of us is? And who knows what tortured her thoughts in the early hours? We can all only deal with the hand of cards we have at the time, and hindsight is a wonderful thing.'

'Yep. But Todd was right, and this is what hurts me the most; I *knew* things weren't right when I came home on leave. Deb was distant, yet smiling, like she was pretending, going through the motions. When I found out she'd kicked Todd out it all made sense to me. I figured she'd been putting up a front so I wouldn't know that he was treating her badly, cos he knew if that had come to light, I'd have killed him.'

'I think so too, and that's rotten, Jack, for her not to have been able to reach out, ask for help or even fully understand what was going on. She must have been so scared. Todd too.'

He nodded, 'I then think when things did start to fall back into place for her, it might have been about revenge and that's a dark thought for me. Todd was right. They were really good together. I can't imagine how she must have felt when she found out he'd cheated.'

'I can.' She gave her husband a wry smile, knowing exactly how it had felt when her first husband, Sonny, was unfaithful and how the revelations had left her reeling. So much so she had jumped on a plane to a place picked randomly on the globe, and had arrived here in Linden Falls, where she met Jack, and the rest, as they say, was history …

'I forget.' He looked at her with a gaze of affection that still had the power to stir desire in her. Not a day went past when she didn't thank her lucky stars. 'I never think of you being married to someone else. I think you've always been mine, even if it took the universe a while to catch up with the fact and put you in my path.'

'I never forget I was married to someone else,' she spoke candidly.

'Is that right?' He looked hurt.

'Because I never ever forget how good I now have it, Jack.' He smiled with something that looked a lot like relief. 'Even arguing with you.' She took a beat, remembering how she and her first husband Sonny would fight, with her pouring out her feelings and he nodding, no doubt with his mind elsewhere. He was disengaged, disinterested, as their marriage disintegrated in front of her eyes. Even arguing with Jack was better, the way he listened, the way he reacted. Their more heated exchanges, while thankfully rare, were always truthful and helped them build a bridge to get where they were going. 'It's so much better, Jack. I know, if we fight, I'm still going to wake up in your arms. I never have that gut-sick worry that everything is so fragile that I have to work every single minute of every single day on holding it all together. With Sonny, I was always kind of aware that one puff of smoke, one click of a finger, or, as it turned out, one wink from a young, pretty woman, and the whole house of cards would be gone. It was as unfulfilling as it was exhausting.'

He reached over and took her hand in his. And there they sat, quietly, letting the dust of discord settle, as their breathing fell in sync and their peace reminded them both that they were one. The cicadas chirped a rhythm that was interspersed by the crackling fire and the occasional pop of a log. It was the very best night music on this beautiful starry, so very starry Vermont night.

'I don't know where to go from here,' her husband broke their quiet with this truth. 'I don't know how to put it all behind me, and the only person who could truly help me make sense of it all is gone.'

'Wherever it is, my love, we go slowly, and we go together. There's no shortcut through the river of grief. It will carry you along on its twisty journey, and there might be days when you get to climb out, sit on the banks and feel the sunshine on your face, but the next you might find yourself dragged beneath the surface, caught up in the weeds and struggling for air; often it will be all you can do to keep your head above the raging torrent. And all this before you try to figure out the questions you will never have the answers to, the misplaced guilt you will wrestle with, and the fact that you'll miss her so much you will be wrapped in sadness.'

'It sounds exhausting,' he echoed.

She squeezed his hand. 'Yep.'

Her phone beeped. She pulled it from her pocket and, with relief, read the message.

'It's from Lindsey. Todd missed his flight and has lost his phone. He called her from the airport; she's on her way to pick him up right now.'

'Good.' He held her eye line. 'How do he and Shaun begin to make up for all those years, Verty? Do you think it's possible?' he asked with so much hope it was painful.

'I think the answer is not to try. I think it's better that everyone looks forward and tries not to analyse all they can't change and everything they can't justify or explain. They need to make the absolute best of what they now have. If that's what they want.'

'When did you get so wise?' He smiled at her.

'When I took a chance and missed *my* flight, jumped in a

cab and came back to this very farm to make a life with the man I loved.'

'I'm sorry.' He reached for her hand. 'I'm sorry for not opening up, for fighting with you … for everything.'

'Don't apologise just yet. You are not out of the woods; when it comes to grief, there will be days ahead when you need to rage at the world, and you can. You and I are each other's haven; you can say and do whatever you need to get through it, Jack. The only thing is I ask—'

'What, love, what do you ask?' He stared at her with longing.

'I ask you never to forget that we are one team. Always one team.'

'One team.' He nodded, and her heart sang with thanks and love for this man, her Jack.

CHAPTER 8

Verity Darby woke on this perfect blue-sky day with a feeling of trepidation lining her gut. Still in her crumpled linen pyjamas, she threw the bedroom window open, and took a moment to appreciate the view, the rolling hills, abundant with elegant clusters of spikey trees, the view down the valley, and, from this vantage point, the beautiful lake in the distance. How she loved this farm, this special, special place. Nearly as much as she loved the man who was at present in the shower, her husband Jack, and the reason she had made Linden Falls her home.

It was hard to believe that it was nearly three months since they had said goodbye to Debra. Today they were holding a memorial lunch in her honour, and it had been her privilege to have been asked to cook it. It had been three months of learning how to be in the bistro without her sister-in-law by her side, three months of Jack mourning his beloved sister, three months of her doing her very best to support him. Three months of rolling with the highs and lows of loss that had the power to pull the rug from under him in the most unexpected of ways. Three months of Arla relaying tales of how Todd and Shaun were getting to know each other from afar, writing letters, chatting on the phone and even the odd FaceTime, where Todd, apparently, did his best to keep it together at no more than the sight of his son. Today was the first time they would meet in person since that rather unsuccessful night at the farm. Today, Todd would get to meet Charlotte and Eva in person, and Verity would get to meet Lindsey.

It was a big day that came with the weight of excited expectation.

Jack came into the room in his towel.

'How are you feeling?' she asked.

'Nervous.' He pulled a face.

'Excited too?'

'A bit.' He smiled. 'I was thinking. I've got pictures in a trunk somewhere of when Todd and I were no more than teenagers. We'd go up to the mountains to camp, drink beer, fish … The drive there in my dad's Chevy was as much a big part of the adventure. We thought we owned that road, driving along in our acid wash jeans, long hair, mirror shades, Van Halen or Def Leppard blaring from the radio.' He stared at her. 'Truth is I've missed him. I haven't allowed myself to miss him in all these years because the person I thought he was didn't exist, and that hurt. But now it's like I can let him back in, not only into my life, but let him back into my memories of us too.'

'I think that's beautiful, Jack.'

'I think you're beautiful.' He reached out and took her hand into his. 'We're good, right?'

'We're always good, my darling.'

It was an unexpected knock on the door that was always, either this early in the day or late at night, a little unnerving.

'Who's that?' she asked, staring at the open window.

He turned to face her, a small smile on his lips, as he grabbed his sweatpants and slipped them on, closely followed by his shirt from the end of the bed.

'You know you always do that?'

'Do what?' She wrinkled her nose.

'You ask who is at the door before I open it.'

'Do I?' She laughed at the absurdity of it.

'Yep. And I always think to myself, if I had such a psychic power, I wouldn't waste it on accurately predicting who was visiting us at some unearthly hour, but I might just have used it to grab a few lottery tickets a while back or to get shares in one of them newfangled companies like *Google* or *Apple* when they started out.'

'You make a good point, but then, if you think about it,' she called after him as he made his way down the stairs with her following, 'if those lucky numbers had come up or your shares had rocketed, we might have a butler or housekeeper and wouldn't *have* to guess who was at the door, wouldn't even have to get up to open the door; we could get Jeeves to do it!'

'Who's Jeeves?' It was his turn to stare at her with a wrinkle to his nose, as he walked briskly along the hallway. It made her laugh.

'Hey, Jack.' She recognised Neva's voice before Jack led her through to the sitting room.

'Neva! Well, this is a lovely surprise; can I get you some tea?' It was always lovely to see their friend, whatever the time.

'No, no. I'm not staying.' The woman held up her hand; in the other, Verity spied an envelope. 'Just wanted to bring you this.'

'What is it?' she asked, as Jack snorted his laughter.

'My wife is so impatient! Apparently, she can't wait for me to open a door or an envelope! She has to know right now!'

She smiled at him; it was true.

Neva jostled the envelope in her hand and took a breath,

'Actually, it's a bit of a strange one; I was asked to bring this over.'

'Right, what is it?' She was curious.

'It's … it's from Debra.' Neva spoke with understandable hesitation.

'Debra?' It seemed that Jack, like her, might have thought he misheard or at least, like her, needed it clarified.

'Yes.' The older woman took her time, her voice soft and low. 'She wanted me to bring it over but was insistent that I wait until the time was right.'

'Until the time was right? What did she mean by that?' Jack looked from Verity to Neva as if wanting to better understand.

Neva took her time.

'I saw her write her wish a while back now, a couple of months before she passed.' It wasn't lost on Verity that this was around the same time her sister-in-law had written to Todd. Had Debra *known* she was sick? It was a sobering thought and raised the question: why would she have kept such a thing from her and Jack? It made little sense. 'I left it on the tree for a few days as I do all the wishes, and, when the weather threatens rain, I gather them in and log them. I saw Debra's wish and would never have mentioned it to her; that's not the way it works. They are often written anonymously and always in confidence. But Debra came to me, asked me to take care of it and deliver it when the time was right. Made me promise. And I believe that the time is now.'

Neva handed the envelope to Jack.

'Thank you, Neva.' Jack took it tentatively into his hands, as if aware of the frailty and magnitude of the contents.

'I'll be off,' Neva thumbed in the direction of the front door, 'Henry is making me eggs.'

'Let him spoil you,' Verity winked at her friend.

'You say that, honey, but you haven't tried Henry's eggs. They're like rubber! See you folks soon.'

With Neva gone, Jack sat at the breakfast bar in the kitchen and turned the envelope over and over as if hoping to find a clue.

'Are you going to open it?' Her impatience was gnawing at her.

Jack slipped his finger under the flap and opened it, carefully pulling the brown luggage label from its confines before laying it flat on the countertop. Verity had of course seen wishes scrawled on these labels before, a whole array of them in fact whenever she walked underneath the spreading linden tree. They were a bright and unique blossom, an important and much-loved feature of this little town. This message, however, was so much more than a dashed-off desire, something written on a whim. Nor was it a comical line captured for the amusement of others, something playful or ridiculous. Nor was it anonymous. It was instead neat, wordy, ordered, and sincere, and it spoke volumes that Debra had asked Neva to see it safely delivered when the time was right.

'What does it say?' she asked gently.

Jack swallowed and took his time, his words forced to navigate the obvious boulder of distress that sat at the base of his throat.

'My name is ...' he coughed and started again, 'My name is Debra May Darby and I have lived here in Linden Falls for a while now. I must confess part of my fascination with the beautiful place is this big old tree that they say has the power to grant wishes.' Jack took a breath, 'Do I believe they can come true? I'm not sure is the honest answer, but I sure hope so. My wish is for forgiveness. I wish for my son, Shaun, to forgive me for sending his daddy away, I wish my brother, Jack,' Jack stopped reading and wiped his eyes, 'my brother, Jack, to forgive me for the loss of his best friend, but, mostly, I wish for forgiveness from Todd who deserved more, deserved better. I believe that with their forgiveness, I will finally be able to forgive myself and be free. This is my greatest wish. Deb x'

Jack buried his face in his hands and sobbed. Verity rushed to him and held him tightly.

'I forgive her, Verty, I do. Of course I forgive her!'

'Hey!' Arla called as she, Shaun, and their two beautiful children walked in.

'Why are you sad?' Charlotte asked Jack directly, while gripping her little sister's hand.

'Do you know, I am not sad!' Jack sat up straight. 'These are happy tears!' He slapped the countertop and went to hold Shaun in an embrace, Arla too.

'Can we go and see your goats?' Charlotte, it seemed had eyed the wily creatures in the enclosure that abutted the yard.

'Sure, you can!' Jack led the way, and the two little girls followed him outside.

'How's he doing?' Shaun whispered.

'Good, good.' She spoke the truth. 'There's something on the countertop for you to read, Todd too when he gets here. How do you feel about seeing him?'

'Looking forward to it, Verity; we have a lot to catch up on.'

'You do, my love.' She squeezed his arm.

'I miss my mom, every day, but it's a complicated legacy she's left behind.'

'Yes, it is, but read what's on the counter, I think it'll help.' She watched him go and lift the envelope and sit down to read ....

It was as Shaun was engrossed in his mother's message that she heard the car pull up, heralding the arrival of Todd and Lindsey. She watched from the window as Jack walked to greet the car. Tears pricked her eyes, as her husband led the charge, putting out his hand to give Todd a warm and welcoming handshake, quite unlike the reluctant hesitancy of his response when the man had arrived before. While shaking hands, Jack reached up and placed his spare arm over Todd's back and there they stood, embracing in a way that was as healing as it was heartwarming.

From where Verity was standing, it looked a whole lot like love ....

Lunch was coming to an end. She and Lindsey had got on famously, Verity liked the woman very much, admired her straight talking, her compassion, and found her tales of life as a middle grade teacher interesting. She looked forward to spending more time in her company as the years rolled on, certain that Jack and Todd would pick up where they left off. Hearing them reminisce and laugh in the way that those close to each other did, with hundreds of small shared private jokes, and that one word that seemed to send them into uncontrollable laughter that meant nothing to anyone else. It was good to see her husband laughing, happy in the moment and with the tension fled from his posture.

Todd was a patient and interested grandpa, chatting to Charlotte and Eva, and asking and answering the many questions as they all tried to learn as much as they could about the other. It was a privilege to witness.

Verity, now thinking about coffee, began to gather the empty plates and was delighted by the compliments on her salmon en croute with watercress sauce, and the lemon tart with limoncello cream for dessert. The little girls had chosen chicken and ice cream and had devoured it with gusto. They were adorable, and now jumped in their chairs, as if boredom was setting in and they were keen to go and explore.

'Can we go find Truffle?' Charlotte asked, sweetly.

'Sure, if that's okay with Aunty Verity?' Arla looked at her for approval.

'Oh, of course!' She knew her pup had taken refuge in the hallway, where she liked to lie on the wooden floor and let the sun coming in through the window streak her fur and warm her bones. The kids were sweet with her, petting her gently and offering lamentations of love in the way that only little ones did. It was quite lovely to see and made her miss Louis more than usual. Sophie's new baby was due in a couple of weeks, and she couldn't wait for news of their arrival when, and she had already told Jack, she'd be jumping straight on a plane!

'I'll go with them.' Arla placed her napkin on the table and went to find her girls.

'I'd like to propose a toast.' Shaun lifted his glass of wine and took a breath; Verity abandoned the plates and sat down. 'Three months without Mom that sometimes feels like three days and other times, three years,' Jack nodded his agreement. 'It's been … a strange time for me, for us all.'

'It sure has.' It was Todd's turn to agree.

Shaun locked eyes with his dad. 'A sad time, of course, but also, in a way, a happy time because I found you, again. And you have found all of us. I love my mom so much, always will. She was the best and, in a strange way, particularly after reading her note, I feel like she set up this new chapter for us, gave us a way forward and that's the most amazing thing. Our story is complicated, confusing sometimes, and truth is I've been as angry as I have been happy. But that's just families, right? Ain't none of us perfect, all of us just trying to figure it out as we go along and make the best decisions we can. Some of those decisions we might wish we had taken differently, but, at the end of the day, it's my belief that there's no point in regret. It only drags you backwards when what you should be doing is looking forward. And that's where we are at, we're looking forward and looking up, just as Mom would want us to.'

Shaun raised his glass in the room where his words had impact, leaving them all a little stunned, a little overcome with emotion. 'To Deb!'

'To Deb!' The echo around the table.

'Are you going to read her note now, Todd?' Lindsey asked with a sense of encouragement, suggesting she knew the man well enough to know that he might be putting it off or was waiting for such an encouragement.

Todd nodded and slowly made his way to the kitchen area. The rest stayed at the table, giving him space and peace to take in the words that had meant so much to Jack and Shaun. It felt odd to make small talk and so they sat in quiet contemplation, until the sound of Todd's tears caused them all to shift in their seats. It was Shaun and Lindsey who went to him, stood either side of him. Shaun's hand on his shoulder, offering love via his proximity.

'I forgive you, Debra May,' Todd spoke aloud, 'I forgive you. I loved you then and I love you always. I know I paid a heavy price, but I know you did too my love, I know you did too.'

Lindsey palmed circles on her husband's back as not a sound shattered the quiet of the room, each person, Verity was sure, running through their own thoughts and feeling sadness in the wake of Todd's words.

She and Jack exchanged a knowing look. It was a moment they would remember.

'If you hadn't spoken to him that day when you found him on the bench by the wishing tree …' he began, his voice no more than a whisper.

Verity shook her head.

'I think we would have reached this point, my love. We might just have taken a different route. But we'd have got here, I have no doubt.'

'Grandpa Todd!' Charlotte's yell shattered the quiet, as she called with enthusiasm. It seemed the novelty of having another grandpa at her beck and call was not waning. 'Come and see what Eva and I have found!'

The little girl ran to him and took his hand as if she had

been doing so her whole life. Todd beamed and stood, smiling at his wife as he allowed himself to be led from the barstool towards the hallway.

'What is it?' Verity was curious as to what the little girls had discovered and were so keen to share.

'You can come too, Aunty Verity! You all can!'

And as was often the way when held in the thrall of children, they all rose and trooped out towards the hallway.

'Look!' Eva pointed to the window where a beautiful insect had landed on the wide, white sill. 'Pretty!'

'It is pretty.' Arla beamed, as Shaun, standing behind his wife, placed his arms around her and held her fast. 'So pretty.'

'That's a Tiger Swallowtail,' Jack leaned over and studied the creature. 'One of the prettiest butterflies of them all, I think.'

Verity stared at the creature, sitting proudly with its wings outstretched, as if delighting in the praise of the whole family and enjoying the feel of the sun on its wings, the bottom of which were edged in the most beautiful shade of cornflower blue.

'What shall we do with her, Grandpa?' Charlotte asked Todd who could barely speak for the emotion that seemed to stopper his words.

'I think, I think we should set her free.' Todd's voice broke.

Jack stepped forward and gently cupped the delicate creature between his big palms where it rested without resistance. As one family, united by grief, emboldened by hope and bound by love, they walked outside into the bright day, as Jack lifted his cupped hands towards the sun.

'Fly high,' Todd whispered into the breeze, 'fly high!'

And they watched, as the beautiful butterfly spiralled up towards the sun … free.

Free at last.

EPILOGUE

If you enjoyed this latest instalment in The Wishing Tree series, you'll love dropping back into the lives of Pam Olson and Steve Turner in Wishful Tails, The Wishing Tree Series, #15. As the cameras roll for Season 2 of the hit home-improvement show Wishes of Home, Pam and Steve dive into their biggest project yet: building the first no-kill animal shelter in their region. With their wedding just around the corner, they find themselves juggling work, wedding plans, and community service, while trying to squeeze in a moment or two of romance.

When a wildfire threatens their community, Pam and Steve rally the town of Linden Falls to come together in the face of disaster. With a nearby animal shelter threatened by the flames, the generous community of Linden Falls bands together to finish the new shelter and take in and treat the four-legged evacuees.

But as the flames subside, the couple faces heartbreak when their wedding venue is destroyed, and Steve's loyal black Lab disappears into the chaos. Join Pam and Steve on a journey of resilience, compassion, and the unwavering hope that, even amidst the darkest of times, miracles can still happen.

Don't miss any books in The Wishing Tree series:

★ Don't miss a Wishing Tree book! ★
Book 1: The Wishing Tree – prologue book
Book 2: I Wish … by Amanda Prowse
Book 3: Wish You Were Here by Kay Bratt
Book 4: Wish Again by Tammy L. Grace
Book 5: Workout Wishes & Valentine Kisses by Barbara Hinske
Book 6: A Parade of Wishes by Camille Di Maio
Book 7: Careful What You Wish by Ashley Farley
Book 8: Gone Wishing by Jessie Newton
Book 9: Wishful Thinking by Kay Bratt
Book 10: Overdue Wishes by Tammy L. Grace
Book 11: A Whole Heap of Wishes by Amanda Prowse
Book 12: Wishes of Home by Barbara Hinske
Book 13: Wishful Witness by Tonya Kappes
Book 14: A Wish for Forgiveness by Amanda Prowse
Book 15: Wishful Tails by Barbara Hinske
Book 16: One More Wish by Tammy L. Grace
Book 17: A Wish in the Wind by Kay Bratt

We also invite you to join us in our My Book Friends group on Facebook. It's a great place to chat about all things bookish and learn more about our founding authors.

ABOUT THE AUTHOR

Amanda Prowse is a multi-million bestselling author and one of the most prolific writers of contemporary fiction in the UK today. She is proud ambassador for The Reading Agency and can be heard weekly on her podcast Chit Chat and All That.

Amanda would love any active readers to join her and fellow founding authors at the fabulous My Book Friends Facebook group, where she hosts a fortnightly session on alternate Fridays.

Printed in Great Britain
by Amazon

45969370R00067